Praise for the Inspector DeKok Series by Baantjer

"Along with such peers as Ed McBain and Georges Simenon, [Baantjer] has created a long-running and uniformly engaging police series. They are smart, suspenseful, and better-crafted than most in the field."
—*Mystery Scene*

"Baantjer's laconic, rapid-fire storytelling has spun out a surprisingly complex web of mysteries."
—*Kirkus Reviews*

"DeKok is a careful, compassionate policeman in the tradition of Maigret; crime fans will enjoy this book."
—*Library Journal*

"DeKok's maverick personality certainly makes him a compassionate judge of other outsiders and an astute analyst of antisocial behavior."
—*The New York Times Book Review*

"It's easy to understand the appeal of Amsterdam police detective DeKok; he hides his intelligence behind a phlegmatic demeanor, like an old dog that lazes by the fireplace and only shows his teeth when the house is threatened."
—*The Los Angeles Times*

Inspector DeKok Series

Titles Available or Forthcoming from Speck Press

DeKok and
Murder by Installment

Number 22 in the Inspector DeKok Series

by

A. C. Baantjer

Translated by H. G. Smittenaar

speck press

denver

Published by: *speck press,* speckpress.com

Printed and bound in the United States of America
ISBN: 1-933108-07-X, ISBN13: 978-1-933108-07-0
Book layout and design by: **CORVUS**, corvusdesignstudio.com

English translation by H. G. Smittenaar copyright © 2007 Speck Press. Translated from *De Cock en moord op termijn,* by Baantjer (Albert Cornelis Baantjer), copyright © 1985 by Uitgeverij De Fontein bv, Baarn, Netherlands. 1st Dutch printing: 1985, 27th Dutch printing: 2006

Library of Congress Cataloging-in-Publication Data
Baantjer, A. C.
[De Cock en moord op termijn. English]
DeKok and murder by installment : number twenty-two in the Inspector Dekok series / by Baantjer ; translated from the Dutch by H.G. Smittenaar.
-- 1st American ed.
p. cm.
"De Cock en moord op termijn."
ISBN-13: 978-1-933108-07-0 (pbk. : alk. paper)
ISBN-10: 1-933108-07-X (pbk. : alk. paper)
1. DeKok, Inspector (Fictitious character)--Fiction. I. Smittenaar, H. G. II. Title.

PT5881.12.A2D5813 2006
839.3'1364--dc22

2006035965

10 9 8 7 6 5 4 3 2 1

1

Inspector DeKok pulled the report closer and started to read. His face was creased with anger. He always considered the writing and reading of reports a waste of time. DeKok's long-time assistant and colleague at Amsterdam's notorious Warmoes Street police station took care of whatever reports were required from the team, but he still had to read them. In the old days, when reports were handwritten, DeKok's were masterful at brevity and succinctness. And they always resulted in a single-sheet conviction, with one carbon copy. With computers, which were supposed to reduce the amount of paperwork, as many as seven or eight copies were produced for every bagatelle.

DeKok never bothered with bagatelles. He solved problems on his beat with a word, a gesture, a hint, and, sometimes, a threat, both as a young, uniformed constable and now as a seasoned inspector in the homicide division. He and Vledder were the only representatives of the homicide division in the station house. The rest of the division was spread out over the other stations, with two, three, and, sometimes, as few as one member of what used to be called the "Murder Brigade."

The report he was reading concerned a just-closed case. It had been a strange and messy one. There was no murder at first. A man had died of natural causes, but those around him wanted to make it appear that he was still alive...for personal gain, of course. The murders started after he died, to protect the secret of the death.

With an exasperated sigh he pushed the papers away from him.

Vledder looked up from his computer screen at the desk next to DeKok.

"Something wrong?"

"No," growled DeKok. "It's just fine. You spelled my name correctly, and as far as I'm concerned you can just finalize it and tell me where to sign."

"But you didn't read it all?"

"Why should I? I know what happened, and I've never known you to make a mistake in a written report."

"That's because you never read them all."

"Well, if you had made a mistake, I'm sure the commissaris or the judge advocate would have let me know." He tossed the papers on Vledder's desk. "This mess has to go."

Vledder shrugged and sorted the papers, glanced over them, and then did something on his keyboard. Multiple copies started to flow out of the printer.

"You know," said DeKok, "I was just thinking. In the old days we wrote reports by hand."

"Yes," said Vledder, who had heard it all before. "Those were the days."

"Indeed," agreed DeKok, ignoring the sarcasm. "The world was less complicated. People generally got along a lot better."

Vledder stood by the printer and started to take the copies out of the tray. He arranged and stapled the sheets together, then started filling the pre-addressed, inter-office envelopes with the report copies.

"But there were murders then, too," Vledder remarked.

"Sure," agreed DeKok, "but not as many. People were still shocked by murder. It was front-page news, day after day. Now a murder gets six lines on page four, third column."

Vledder smiled.

"Well, don't worry about it. The job is done." He gathered the completed envelopes and tossed them into his out basket.

Jan Kuster, the watch commander, entered the detective room and walked over to DeKok's desk.

"Downstairs I have an eighteen-year-old boy with two ten-ounce packages of cocaine."

"So," said DeKok, looking at him. "That's a job for narcotics."

Kuster sighed deeply.

"I know that. But you're the only detectives here—and besides the cocaine, he has some rolls of money, a hundred thousand Euros altogether."

DeKok looked surprised.

"What?"

"He's carrying a hundred thousand Euros in four plastic bags, each with twenty-five thousand. The cops who arrested him on Seadike found the money when they frisked him at the station. It was taped around his waist."

"Strange."

"That's what I said," nodded Kuster. "But according to him it was the best way to defeat pickpockets."

"What else did he have on him?"

"There wasn't anything out of the ordinary...a wallet with a few hundred in it, a driver's license, and the registration papers for a Porsche."

Vledder whistled.

"That's an expensive, fast car."

"Is that like the cars the state police use?" asked DeKok, who professed to know little, or nothing, about cars.

"Yes," answered Kuster, "barely six months old."

DeKok rubbed the side of his nose.

"The money...is it real? I mean, not counterfeit?"

Kuster shook his head.

"No way it's fake. These are blemished bills. They've been a circulation for awhile, and are undoubtedly genuine."

"And how does he explain the money?"

The watch commander hooked a chair with his leg and sat down.

"He doesn't explain it. He refuses to say anything. But there has to be something wrong. I mean, eighteen years old! That's no age to—"

"Is he a dealer?"

Kuster shrugged.

"I don't think so. And he doesn't look like a junkie, either. I checked with headquarters. No record. He's never been in contact with the police or the courts."

DeKok shook his head.

"A boy with a clean record has a hundred thousand on his stomach. In this crazy business you run into all sorts of things." He leaned back in his chair and sighed deeply. "All right, bring him up...with his cocaine and his money. We'll look into it and see what we can find out."

The young man was neatly dressed. He wore a sporty, dark-blue blazer and a light-blue, sharply creased pair of trousers. His blonde hair was cut into a crew cut, and his slightly tanned face was dominated by a set of clear blue eyes.

The gray sleuth leaned forward; his lips formed a smile.

"My name is DeKok," he said in a friendly tone of voice, "with a kay-oh-kay. With whom do I have the pleasure?"

"Casper, Casper Hoogwoud. It's already in the report they filled out downstairs." It sounded like an accusation.

DeKok raised his hands in defense.

"Please, spare me the mention of reports." Then he smiled again. "Casper Hoogwoud," he repeated, "a nice name."

"You think so?"

DeKok nodded agreeably.

"Yes, it sounds nice. I always feel that a nice name means a nice person."

The compliment did not get the reaction DeKok had hoped for. Casper Hoogwoud did not seem to soften. He looked suspiciously at the inspector.

"Surely you don't expect me to be *nice* to you?"

"But why not?"

The young man shook his head resolutely.

"I don't feel the need. I have been robbed abruptly of my freedom and they have taken my money away."

"Your money?"

"Certainly."

"How did you come by that much money?"

Casper remained obstreperous.

"I didn't steal it."

DeKok spread his hands, asking for understanding.

"There are many ways, apart from stealing, to obtain money illegally. The law books are full of them."

The young man waved nonchalantly.

"I'm not interested in your laws," he said haughtily. He pointed at the bags of money on the desk. "That's my property. You are free to think I have obtained it in some criminal manner, but unless you can prove that, the money is mine."

DeKok smiled.

"You forget the inquisition."

Hoogwoud looked momentarily confused.

"What inquisition?"

"The Belastingdienst. Taxes, Casper. They still maintain the inquisition principle of reverse proof. You're guilty until you prove yourself innocent."

The young man frowned.

"You mean that I would have to prove to them how I obtained the money?"

"Yes, and you can count on a sizeable assessment."

Casper Hoogwoud moved in his chair.

"I made it gambling."

"Illegal gambling?"

"Yes."

DeKok pursed his lips.

"I presume that you will not, as a matter of principle, tell me the name of the illegal gambling house?"

"You presume correctly," grinned Hoogwoud.

DeKok rubbed his face with his hand. The question-and-answer game amused him. The young man was not unsympathetic. On the contrary, he felt Casper Hoogwoud, despite his tender years, showed a refreshing amount of maturity.

"Are you an addict?"

"No."

DeKok pretended surprise.

"What about the cocaine?"

"It's for my brother."

"He's an addict?"

"Yes."

"Why doesn't your brother buy his own drugs?"

"Marcel is ill."

DeKok again pursed his lips.

"Too ill to buy his own drugs?"

Casper did not answer immediately. For the first time he seemed to lose some of his confidence. His tongue touched dry lips.

"Marcel has AIDS."

With Casper Hoogwoud squeezed into the back seat, the battered police VW pulled away from the station house. Vledder was driving, as usual, and DeKok was slumped in the seat next to him. He turned to look at the young man in the back seat. Casper had regained his self-confidence and stared back without expression.

"I protest your keeping my money." His tone was even. "I don't think it's safe. It wouldn't be the first time something disappeared from a police station."

DeKok made a helpless gesture.

"I have kept strictly to the letter of the law and the regulations. I've given you a receipt for the money *and* the cocaine. Tomorrow I will contact the judge advocate or, rather, my commissaris will do it. In any case the judge advocate will decide what happens next with the money. I can't take your statement about gambling profits seriously. For the moment I will have to assume the money was from, or meant for, drug dealing."

"That is merely an assumption…and the wrong one at that," replied Hoogwoud.

"Exactly, it's an assumption and it may very well be the wrong one. Regardless, based on that assumption, I obtained a warrant to search your house. The narcotics laws don't even require me to do that."

"You think you'll find drugs in our house?" grinned Casper.

DeKok shrugged his shoulders.

"I cannot exclude the possibility. But in fact, I'm more interested in the medical condition of your brother, Marcel. And perhaps I'll have an opportunity to speak to your parents."

Casper Hoogwoud momentarily pressed his lips together. His attitude became one of protest.

"My brother and I don't live at home, any longer. My father is an old-fashioned patriarch with outdated ideas about raising a family. My brother could no longer live under his regime."

DeKok noticed the bitter tone. His face showed a sudden interest.

"And what about you?"

"What?"

"Were you also unable to live any longer under your father's regime?"

Hoogwoud lowered his head slightly.

"Father is a despot. When it became possible to move in with my brother, I did. Only my sister still lives at home."

"And your mother?"

The young man stared into the distance with a dreamy look in his eyes.

"Mother passed away long ago," he said softly. "She died when I was still very small. I have no conscious memory of her. In fact, I only know her from a photograph. It shows her as a fragile little woman in the doorway of our house."

They drove on in silence. DeKok faced forward and slumped back in the seat, his much abused little hat pulled down to his eyes. He glanced out of the window from underneath the brim and recognized the arcade of Town Hall Street. He did not feel comfortable in this new position and pressed himself upright. Then he turned again toward Casper.

"How old is Marcel?"

"Thirty-six."

"Quite a bit older than you."

Hoogwoud nodded vaguely.

"But we get along just fine. He treats me like an adult...not like his kid brother, in case that's what you're thinking."

DeKok ignored the remark.

"Does your brother know you walk around with all that money?"

"Yes, he does."

DeKok feigned surprise.

"And he doesn't object?"

Casper Hoogwoud lifted his chin defiantly.

"It is *my* money, *my* behavior, *my* business. Marcel respects that."

DeKok nodded to himself, but he couldn't think of an explanation for such a large amount of cash. He had still not succeeded in breaking through the stiff reserve of the young man.

"Shouldn't Marcel be treated in a hospital?"

The young man sighed.

"That would indeed be better for him, but Marcel doesn't want it. He doesn't like hospitals, or doctors. He mistrusts what he calls 'those murderers in white coats.'"

"Murderers?"

"One of Marcel's expressions," smiled Casper.

Vledder stopped the car at the side of the road.

"We're not there yet, but I have a parking spot here."

They exited the car and closed the doors. DeKok pulled up the collar of his raincoat. The evening air was chilly, and it had started to rain.

When they reached the house, Casper took a key from his pocket and opened the door.

He preceded the inspectors through a long, wide corridor to a spacious room with a high ceiling. A man reclined on a sofa. His eyes were closed. Casper walked toward him.

"Marcel, here are two gentlemen from the police."

DeKok looked down at the man on the sofa. The expression on his face and the pallor of his skin concerned him. Casper shook the man's shoulder.

"Marcel."

There was an undertone of fear in his voice. He again took the man by the shoulder and shook more vigorously. DeKok took him by the arm.

"Leave him," he said softly.

The young man looked up at him. There was confusion in his bright blue eyes.

"Marcel," he whispered.

DeKok's face expressed compassion.

"Marcel is dead," he said.

2

DeKok pressed his little hat more firmly on his head. The light rain had developed into a full-blown storm. Ghostly shards of clouds chased each other in the pale moonlight. The slender light poles swayed in the wind, and the sound of slate being ripped off a roof echoed around them. Almost crouching against the fury of the storm, DeKok and Vledder reached the VW. The vehicle was rocking on its springs. They hurried inside, but Vledder did not drive away.

He looked askance at DeKok, who stared somberly through the windshield. The old sleuth tried to grasp what they had learned so far. They had an eighteen-year-old young man with a hundred thousand Euros, at least that much in cocaine, and an obscenely expensive car. The same young man leads them to a richly furnished residence with a dead brother. The combination did not please him.

"Marcel didn't look like a homosexual."

DeKok looked at Vledder, his thoughts interrupted.

"Why do you think he was gay?"

"Well, he had AIDS."

DeKok shook his head.

"You need to be mindful of making such blind assumptions, Dick."

"Well, I...eh..." stammered Vledder.

DeKok interrupted rather brusquely.

"Don't try to classify people just by their looks. It can't be done. The most pious looking priest can be a child molester and an effeminate man may very well be happily married with a dozen children. Many ladies are whores and many whores are ladies." Then he smiled and added, "And some experienced police officers are prone to snap judgments."

Vledder had the grace to blush, but did not respond. For awhile the two remained seated, watching the storm. Then Vledder started the engine and pulled carefully away from the curb, avoiding scattered trash cans.

"You want to go back to the station?"

"Certainly," nodded DeKok. "But try to avoid the canals as much as possible. If we do get blown off the road, I'd just as soon stay dry."

Vledder laughed, and he did avoid the canals until they reached Rembrandt Square. It looked deserted. The prostitutes and their prospective clients had all been blown inside. They reached the Amstel by way of Half Moon Alley.

"Are we pursuing this case?" asked Vledder.

"I don't think so," answered DeKok. "Casper will get his day in court for the cocaine. His brother died a natural death."

"And that's it?"

DeKok made an irritated gesture.

"I still have the hundred thousand Euros in a plastic bag. I really don't feel like giving them back to Casper. But, if the judge advocate finds no indication the money has been obtained illegally, we'll have to return it."

Vledder grinned.

"The judge advocate can also inform the IRS. They'll be there at the crack of dawn to take possession."

"There is always a chance, of course."

The young inspector frowned.

"I still think," Vledder said thoughtfully, "the money may have come from sort of drug deal, something Casper did just before he was arrested."

DeKok nodded slowly.

"But we'll never prove it. That's the problem. You're right, though, in the drug trade they don't deal with checks and credit cards." He smiled sadly. "Unless you inherit large capital, there's no honest way to get rich in The Netherlands. There's no way...certainly not at age eighteen. Besides, who straps money to their waist?"

"Maybe he did inherit it," offered Vledder.

DeKok snorted.

"His father is a greenskeeper at a golf course. I don't know exactly what that entails, but it doesn't seem as though it would make you rich."

"What about a sugar daddy?"

DeKok ignored the suggestion, hating that expression. He pressed himself higher in his seat.

"Casper Hoogwoud seems to be a nice, charming young man." His tone changed, becoming more incisive. "But that is a false picture. I sense he's a devilishly dangerous individual, who has acquired a harsh mentality. He dares to play dangerous games. Tomorrow I'll have a talk with narcotics. The fact that he doesn't appear in our records means nothing."

"You mean he could have been in the sights of the authorities several times, but there was no proof?" asked Vledder, keeping his eyes on the road.

"Exacto, as Little Lowee likes to say."

The VW had reached Dam Square. From the car they could see white caps on the usually placid waters of the Damrak. The tour boats tugged at their moorings. Crewmembers crawled over them, checking the lines and lowering additional old tires over the sides to absorb shock as the boats slammed against each other.

They entered Warmoes Street. Vledder parked the car in front of the station house with a sigh and shut off the engine.

The wind practically pushed them through the doors of the station. Just inside they stopped to shake the rain off their coats and DeKok shook out his hat.

Kuster came from behind the counter. The watch commander seemed agitated.

"Well, for once I don't blame you for keeping your radio off. There is enough static to blast your ears. Nonetheless I do need you."

"What for?"

"We have a possible murder. I've sent a patrol car to the location, but it's your bailiwick."

"Where?"

"Emperor's Canal, near Hearts Street. They found a man in front of the door of a lawyer's office."

"Dead?"

Kuster nodded.

"Somebody bashed in his skull."

When Vledder opened the car door he cursed from the bottom of his heart. His face was red. He sat down and closed the door with a bang.

"Two corpses in one night…and *what* a night. It is just too much," he growled. "We don't even have time to think!"

DeKok grinned broadly.

"And I thought you found police work the best job in the world?"

The young inspector nodded with vigor.

"It is." He started the engine, "It just gives me the jitters when too much comes at me all at once."

DeKok's face was expressionless.

"Contact some future killers," he said evenly. "Perhaps they'll spread out their activities over a more convenient schedule."

Vledder did not look pleased.

"Go fly a kite," he responded.

"Not in this weather," said DeKok amiably as he slid down in the seat. "Just take it easy," he added. "Dead is dead. We can't change that and, besides, nobody will hear your siren in this weather."

Vledder unwillingly reduced his speed and shut off the siren.

"I would like to get a little sleep tonight," he muttered, disgruntled.

DeKok pushed his hat farther down over his eyes.

"Youth," he mused.

Eventually they reached Emperors Canal. On the bridge to Hearts Street was a patrol car. Vledder passed it and parked on Emperors Canal, under the trees. The storm had not abated.

A young, uniformed constable approached DeKok. The visor of his cap was pulled down over his eyes.

"I think it's him, himself," he roared above the noise of the storm.

"Who?"

"The dead man."

DeKok smiled mildly.

"Do you mind if I say that I don't understand what you're talking about?"

The young constable looked momentarily embarrassed, but then he began to grin.

"I think," he said more calmly, "the dead man on the stoop is the lawyer who has his office here. He may have been attacked while he was trying to open the door. His keys are still in his hand."

DeKok placed a hand briefly on the constable's shoulder.

"That's a lot clearer," he praised. "Has the herd been alerted?"

"Yes, the watch commander told us over the radio."

DeKok followed the constable to the house. The doorway was recessed and there was a small portico at the top of the stoop. The legs of the dead man protruded from the niche, wet with rain. With a flashlight in one hand, DeKok kneeled next to the corpse. He discovered a deep, gaping wound on the back of the head. Dark red clots of blood and other matter stuck to the hairs at the nape of the neck.

Vledder leaned closer.

"Attacked from the back."

DeKok nodded slowly.

Next to the head of the dead man was a pair of spectacles with expensive, gold frames. One lens was broken. The victim clenched a leather case in his right fist. Some keys protruded from the case.

DeKok's knees creaked as he rose. With the flashlight he looked at the inner walls of the doorway.

"A single blow," he murmured.

"What was that?" asked Vledder.

"The first blow was the only one the killer delivered. If he had struck more than once, there would have been blood on the walls." He handed the flashlight to Vledder. "Take a good look yourself. My eyes aren't what they used to be."

While Vledder looked closely at the walls, DeKok looked down upon the dead man. He estimated him to be about fifty years old. And he won't get any older, he thought. The man was dressed in an expensive, dark-blue suit. DeKok could just see a pearl-gray necktie and diamond stick pin. There was no overcoat.

The old inspector beckoned to the young constable.

"Try the hoods of some of the parked cars. Maybe there's one that is still warm."

"The victim's car?"

DeKok nodded.

"Yes. And write down the make, model, and registration of all cars that are still warm."

The constable disappeared in the rain.

Vledder tapped DeKok on the shoulder.

"You're right. There is no blood spatter and the door hasn't been touched—no signs of anyone breaking in." He aimed the beam of the flashlight at the imposing brass nameplate next to the door. "J. O. B. Abbenes, Attorney-at-Law, Solicitor-Barrister," he read out loud. He aimed the beam at the victim. "You think it's him?"

"It seems likely. As soon as Weelen has taken his pictures, we can see if there are any papers on him."

"Abbenes...ever heard of him?"

DeKok shrugged.

"It doesn't ring a bell."

Vledder smirked.

"J. O. B.," he said. "What kind of parents would call their son *Job*?"

DeKok gave him a chiding look.

"The Biblical Job was a very devout man."

"But he lived on a manure pile."

DeKok ignored the remark. The car from the dactyloscopic service pulled up. In the distance they heard the siren and saw the lights of an ambulance. Before long the *thundering herd*, DeKok's special name for the small army of specialists and crime scene investigators, would arrive. DeKok always tried to get away before that happened. He liked to talk to Weelen, the photographer; Kruger, the fingerprint expert; and the coroner. But the rest, especially the high-ranking officers who always gathered at a murder scene, left him cold. He still clung to his old habits when a photographer, a coroner, and, sometimes, a fingerprint expert were usually the only help a homicide investigator would have. After they did their work, he was on his own. He still was not sure all the modern assistance of crime labs, profilers, and sterile CSIs was any help. Murder, he felt, was a very personal thing. Murder involved people, not machines or analytical technology. He had always been able to solve all of his cases without this so-called assistance.

Vledder pointed at the corpse.

"Why would a man go to his office at this time of night in this weather?"

"That, Dick, is exactly what I would like to know."

This time, DeKok had been unable to escape before the full herd arrived. He sat down in the patrol car until they left. Vledder gave the instructions to Bram Weelen, the photographer. The coroner was a young man, obviously new to the job. Since he was not old Dr. Koning, DeKok had not bothered with him either. Kruger took one look at the crime scene and told Vledder he could do no good with all the brick and rainwater all over the place. He waved at DeKok from the patrol car as he hastily left. The high-ranking officers took a quick look at the scene, also retreating to their cars. Only four or five crime scene investigators, impressive in their white suits, spent another half hour looking for things that weren't there.

When everybody, except the morgue attendants, had left, DeKok finally emerged from the patrol car and kneeled once more next to the corpse. He retrieved a wallet and a pocket agenda from the corpse. These he handed to Vledder. Then he pried the key case from between the fingers of the dead man. He straightened up and nodded at the morgue attendants who were patiently waiting in their van.

The storm seemed to have increased in ferocity. DeKok pressed his little hat firmer on his head and looked at the elm trees swaying in the wind.

Vledder watched as the morgue attendants placed the corpse on a stretcher and hastily fastened the belts to keep it in place. They did not bother with a sheet or a body bag. They just wanted to get out of the rain as soon as possible.

DeKok watched as they struggled with the stretcher in the wind, finally shoving it into the back of the van. They slammed the doors and got into the cabin. When the red taillight disappeared, DeKok turned to Vledder.

"Let's get out of here." He looked up at the trees. "I don't trust those old trees in this kind of weather."

At Warmoes Street, Jan Kuster had been replaced by Meindert Post, the Urker watch commander. He looked at the clock.

"You guys are pretty late," he roared. Post always seemed to talk at the top of his voice.

DeKok shrugged.

"It didn't go smoothly."

Post grinned. He knew what that meant.

"Did Kuster leave any notes about the previous case?"

"Of course, what do you think? You're asking about the cocaine possession?"

"Yes, the suspect is Casper Hoogwoud."

Post checked the records.

"That's right. But I don't know what happened to him."

DeKok waved at the door.

"His brother passed away. We left him at home."

"And what do you want me to do about him now?" asked Meindert Post.

"Whatever you do in a situation like this. It's not our case. Narcotics will probably contact you. We have a homicide on our hands."

"Easy for you," mocked Post.

"We'll give you a report about the murder before we leave. We still have to write it up."

"You mean, Vledder has to write it up," said Post, "I know the last time *you* wrote a report. I still have it. It's handwritten and the paper has yellowed over time."

DeKok turned on his heels.

Vledder grinned at Post and followed his partner up the stairs.

In the deserted detective room, DeKok fell into his chair with a sigh. He tossed his hat in the direction of the peg on the wall but missed as usual. Vledder handed him the items taken from the corpse, went over to his own desk, and switched on his computer.

"Is the name good?" he asked.

DeKok nodded, taking a driver's license out of the wallet.

"His full name is Jacob Otto Bernard Abbenes. His residence is at Minerva Lane 783 in Amsterdam."

The phone on DeKok's desk started to ring.

Vledder pushed a button on his own phone, picked it up, and listened. Without saying a word he replaced the receiver after a few seconds.

"And who was that?" asked DeKok.

"I don't know."

"But there was someone on the line?"

"A woman," nodded Vledder.

"And?"

"She only said a few words: 'Marcel has been murdered.'"

3

DeKok was seated near the window of the streetcar. The storm of the previous night had caused a considerable amount of destruction. The sidewalks were covered with smashed roof tiles and broken branches. On Roses Canal the scaffolding in front of a building had collapsed and blocked the road. Some of the debris was still in the water of the canal. DeKok wondered briefly why overhead electric feed wires for the streetcars were still intact. This most controversial of all Amsterdam vehicles was able to proceed unhindered.

DeKok alighted on Station Square. Usually he walked from there with the stream of commuters to the Damrak. But this time he passed the bus depot and entered the Metro station. He passed by the trains to the exit on Prince Henry Quay. He wanted to take a look at old St. Nicholas Church. He loved the ramshackle old tower and nursed some fond memories of Pastor Aarts, whom he had met several times in the past. The old shepherd's outdated, naive sympathy for people had always touched him. Although his "congregation" consisted almost entirely of criminals, prostitutes, and brothel keepers, the old man refused to think ill of anyone.

He eventually arrived on Warmoes Street by way of St. Olof's Gate. Whistling an off-key Christmas carol, he entered the station house, waved at the watch commander, and climbed the stairs to the floor above. He found Vledder seated behind his computer in the detective room. DeKok nodded to some of the other detectives as he found his way to the windows near the back of the crowded room. Vledder looked ragged. DeKok looked at him with surprise.

"Did you get any sleep?"

Vledder took his hands off the keyboard and yawned heavily.

"You know what time I finally got home? Four o'clock. At that hour I'm better off forgetting everything about sleep...I'm too wound up." He gave DeKok a jealous look. "What about you?"

DeKok winked.

"I first took a large glass of cognac to warm me on the inside. Then I went to bed and snuggled close to my wife." He grinned boyishly. "That warmed the outside."

"And you slept?"

"Like a log."

The young inspector waved languidly at the chair next to his desk.

"This morning I also had to cope with Commissaris Buitendam."

DeKok narrowed his eyes.

"He made an appearance this early? And what did our respected chief have to say?"

"I was surprised to see him. He was rather nervous, confused, and upset. He made remarks concerning the sparse wording of the report. It was just too meager, he said." Vledder paused. "Not enough information, no detail," he added.

"What details? What more did he want?"

"He was talking about the murder of Abbenes, the lawyer."

DeKok gave his younger colleague a searching look.

"And that is why he left home so early?"

"I definitely got that impression."

"But how did he know about the murder? We hadn't informed him. And there was nothing in the papers about it."

"Somebody called him."

"Who?"

"A woman, an unknown woman."

DeKok sighed.

"Again a woman."

Vledder nodded and lifted a piece of paper from the desk.

"She said: 'Abbenes is dead, not because of your righteousness, but because of mine.'"

Commissaris Buitendam, the tall, stately chief of Warmoes Street Station, waved a slender, well-manicured hand.

"Please, sit down, DeKok," he said in his aristocratic voice.

DeKok gave the commissaris a long look. The man looked tired. His long face with its sunken cheeks had almost no color. His eyes looked dull. The sight moved DeKok to pity. The commissaris, he thought, not for the first time, should have been a diplomat. He should have been transferred to headquarters long since. The bureaucracy there was much more suited to the man than the hustle and bustle of the busiest police station in Europe.

With a shrug, DeKok sat down.

The commissaris sat back in his chair and coughed delicately.

"In a little while," he began, "I'll have to inform the judge advocate, Mr. Schaap, that Mr. Abbenes is dead, the victim of a violent assailant. I read your notes in the log and I read your report. I must say, the language was unusually terse."

DeKok again shrugged his shoulders.

"I am sorry," he said placatingly. "There was little to report last night. A man died on a portico with his skull smashed. There's no more."

"A robbery?"

DeKok shook his head.

"I did not get that impression. His wallet, with money, was still in his pocket. He still had all his jewelry—expensive watch, rings, diamond stick pin."

Buitendam spread his hands in a gesture of surrender.

"What could the motive have been?"

DeKok smiled.

"If you know, I'd be obliged."

The commissaris ignored the remark. He moved in his chair.

"Mr. Abbenes," he said carefully, "was an important man. He was very influential. His death or, rather, the manner of his death, will cause a lot of commotion and curiosity. Therefore I want to advise you to be very careful in your investigations."

DeKok grinned briefly.

"I usually am."

Buitendam's face became stern.

"It would be better," he said evenly, "if we dropped

this sore subject. There have been instances in the past..."
He sighed and did not complete the sentence. "Seriously,
DeKok, Mr. Abbenes had relationships in the highest
circles. I would not at all be surprised if The Hague were
to take an interest."

"He moved in government circles?"

"Exactly."

DeKok pulled back his lower lip and let it plop back. He
saw the annoyed look on the commissarial face and stopped
the unsavory habit at once.

"I never knew Abbenes as a lawyer. I understand he also
acted as a barrister?"

Buitendam nodded slowly.

"Only in rare, special cases...cases that interested him
somehow. Abbenes was a rich man. He could afford to
pick and choose his clients. Mostly he acted as a solicitor
in civil cases."

DeKok stared into the distance for awhile. An innocent
smile played around his lips.

"My old mother," he said, reminiscing, "never had
much truck with lawyers. She used to say: 'The lawyer
makes his cash from the stubborn, the nuts, and the rash.'"
The gray sleuth drove the memory of his mother from his
thoughts and focused again on the commissaris. "I heard
from Vledder you received a phone call last night?"

"Yes."

"At what time?"

"I think about four o'clock."

"Think? Didn't you look at the clock?" asked DeKok,
irked.

"No."

"It was a woman?"

"Yes."

"Was she young, old?"

"I couldn't say."

"Could she have called earlier?"

"What do you mean?"

"The time could be important. Is it possible you may not have heard the phone earlier in the evening?"

"No. I have a phone next to the bed."

DeKok leaned forward.

"What exactly did she say? What were her exact words?"

Buitendam closed his eyes for a moment.

"She said, 'Abbenes is dead, not because of your righteousness, but because of mine.'"

"Did she have an accent?"

The commissaris shook his head.

"I did not notice one."

"Where was the emphasis?"

"Emphasis?"

DeKok acted distraught.

"The emphasis," he said impatiently. "What did she emphasize? Was it *your* and *mine*, or was it the word *righteousness*?"

"That, eh, that. I don't remember that."

DeKok pressed his lips together. Then he took a deep breath.

"I had hoped," he said angrily, "that a commissaris of police would be—" He was interrupted.

Buitendam stood up. His face was red and his lips quavered. He made a theatrical gesture toward the door.

"OUT!" he roared.

Vledder shook his head.

"You just couldn't control yourself, could you?" There was censure in his voice. "I think you do it on purpose. You elevate his blood pressure every time. It's sadistic—you should watch it."

DeKok spread both hands in a gesture of innocence.

"I could not help it. I really did not intend to make him angry. He looked so wan and tired, I had firmly decided to treat him with consideration and respect. I just lost my temper when he knew so little about the phone call."

"Well, at least he remembered the text," added Vledder. "But that was about all."

"You think the message means something?"

DeKok nodded thoughtfully.

"Of course it means something. Righteousness is another word for *justice*. But don't ask me for an interpretation. There's not much sense to make out of it. But it does seem as if that woman disagrees with the kind of *justice* we practice."

"And is in favor of her own brand of righteousness?"

"Something like that, yes. Although I still don't know what that would entail." He sighed. "But one thing is for sure, she knew last night that Abbenes had left this world."

Vledder's eyes lit up.

"You're right, but how?"

DeKok smiled.

"It would be really nice if I could answer that at this moment."

He rubbed his nose with his little finger.

"When did you tell the Minerva Lane watch commander to inform Abbenes' wife about her husband's death?"

Vledder thought a moment.

"I contacted him not long after we returned from Emperors Canal, about quarter past three. It was after our anonymous female caller."

"In that case we can take it as written that Abbenes' wife would have been informed not much later than four o'clock in the morning."

Vledder looked shocked.

"You think the mysterious female on the phone was his wife?"

DeKok stared out of the window. He did not answer at once.

"Whoever the woman was," he said finally, "we can be sure she was close to the murderer."

They remained silent for a long time. DeKok half closed his eyes and seemed to doze off. Vledder half-heartedly made some entries in his computer. Outside an early drunk yelled something intelligible; they heard Moshe, the herring man, reply in kind. Perhaps the drunk was obstructing the path of his cart as he maneuvered it down the street.

Vledder finally broke the silence.

"While you were with commissaris, I talked to Dr. Rusteloos." The young man looked at his watch. "He wants to start the autopsy in about an hour."

DeKok nodded his understanding.

"Are you going?"

"Yes, because you don't want to."

"Ask him if he can say anything about the weapon that was used. And get some information about AIDS."

The young inspector raised his eyebrows.

"Are we going to get involved with the Hoogwoud case after all?"

DeKok shrugged. "Marcel Hoogwoud died a natural death. There is no reason to suspect a crime."

"How do you explain the phone call?"

"I don't know, is that a reason to confiscate the corpse?"

Vledder shook his head.

"It's just a bit remarkable *that* phone call also came from a woman." He looked at his partner. "Isn't there somebody else who can tell us about AIDS?"

"Why?"

"You can hardly have a conversation with Dr. Rusteloos. His hearing is rapidly going."

DeKok laughed.

"Then you'll just have to speak louder."

He stood up and walked over to get his coat and hat. Vledder called from his desk.

"Where are you going?"

The gray sleuth half turned.

"I'm going to continue an old detective tradition."

"And what is that?"

"I'm going to express my sympathy to the widow concerning the loss of her husband."

4

DeKok looked at the house number on Minerva Lane and let his glance stray to the nameplate. *J. O. B. Abbenes*, it stated in elegant copperplate on a white enamel background. He pressed the brass button mounted below the sign.

It took at least a minute. Then the door was carefully opened by a tall, distinguished lady in a high-buttoned black dress.

"Mrs. Abbenes?"

"Indeed."

It sounded forceful.

DeKok politely lifted his hat and made a courteous bow.

"My name is DeKok," he said hoarsely, "with a kay-oh-kay. I'm an inspector attached to Warmoes Street Police Station, and I would like to talk to you concerning the passing of your husband. I have been assigned the investigation."

Mrs. Abbenes nodded her understanding. She stepped aside and gestured permission to enter. After she had closed the front door behind him, she preceded him to a spacious living room with solid leather furniture.

"Please sit down."

The old inspector lowered himself into an easy chair, unbuttoned his coat, and placed his hat on the floor next to the chair.

"I understand," he began hesitantly, "this must have been a shock for you. I can imagine how difficult it is for you to talk about this."

She seated herself on a straight-backed chair across from him. She remained stiff and erect, her knees closely pressed together.

"I don't mind talking about it," she said cheerfully. "The shock wasn't all that great. Jacob...Jacob was my husband, in a legal sense. Not much more than that."

For just a moment DeKok's eyebrows rippled across his forehead. In an instant it seemed two hairy caterpillars crossed above his eyes. The woman looked startled, but regained her composure almost immediately, as if she had only imagined what she had seen. It gave DeKok time to gather his thoughts and take a new direction. The answer had been unexpected.

"But, eh, you lived here together?"

Mrs. Abbenes nodded slowly.

"That's right, yes. This was Jacob's residence. But to share a home is not the same thing as living together." She paused while a slight smile fled across her lips. "I get the impression that I am confusing you."

"I confess, a bit."

She laughed out loud.

"I didn't think experienced inspectors from Warmoes Street, of all places, could be easily shocked."

DeKok looked at her. When she laughed she had a pleasant face with laugh wrinkles around the eyes. He cocked his head to one side.

"You'll have to forgive me," he said apologetically. "Your attitude, your manner, surprised me. I had prepared myself to meet a grieving widow, sorrowing for the loss of her husband. I was prepared to offer my condolences."

The laugh faded away.

"You must not think his death leaves me cold. It isn't that way at all. Perhaps the pain will come later." She sighed deeply. "Jacob and I grew apart over the years."

"But you're not divorced."

Mrs. Abbenes shook her head.

"I think that we both lacked the courage to make a final break."

"How did the rift come about?"

She did not answer at once. She lowered her head and clasped her hands together on her knees.

"It happened gradually. The breach would widen every time I discovered another of Jacob's character flaws."

"What kind of flaws?"

"Mostly it was small aggravations—sly arrogance, nasty habits. I could not agree with the way Jacob manipulated people. I rebelled when he talked about people as though they were marionettes. He controlled others like wooden dolls, whose strings he could pull. He talked about sheep that needed to be led."

DeKok looked at her sharply.

"Was his killer one of the marionettes?"

Mrs. Abbenes shrugged.

"Perhaps…perhaps one of his dolls realized he'd sold his soul."

"And no longer obeyed?"

She nodded.

"It is a possibility."

DeKok rested his chin on his fist.

"Have you any suggestions as to the direction I should follow to find the perpetrator?"

She shook her head.

"Through his practice Jacob knew so many people. He was involved in so many activities, some that could not stand the light of day…that's why the murder did not completely surprise me. Plenty of people had motives. Jacob was almost permanently surrounded by a cloud of conflict."

DeKok smiled at the description.

"Why did he go to his office in the middle of the night, during such abysmal weather?"

"He had made an appointment."

"With whom?"

She looked at him. Her face had changed expression. The laugh wrinkles had disappeared. For the first time she showed some sadness, a silent sorrow.

"That I don't know," she said softly. "It was sometime between one and two in the morning. I was in bed and heard the telephone ring. I could not follow the conversation…didn't try, really. Toward the end Jacob said something like: 'All right, then, come to my office.' Shortly thereafter he left."

"Without telling you?"

Mrs. Abbenes shook her head.

"As I told you, we just lived together in the same house."

DeKok leaned forward.

"If you try," he cajoled, "maybe you can remember something else about that phone call?"

She stood up.

"I will try," she said. "Although I'm afraid…" She did not complete the sentence. After a brief pause she continued. "Jacob was not his usual self the last few months." It sounded analytical. "He was different, less sure of himself, irritable, nervous."

DeKok picked up his hat from the floor and stood up.

"Do you know why?"

She walked slowly to the door.

"Women," she said hesitantly, "women often have a sharp instinct for moods. I think his bad disposition had something to do with a fraud case he had taken on. A young man had cheated a bank and some bothersome clients were involved."

"Did your husband discuss that with you?"

She stopped and shook her head.

"No, I just caught snatches of a conversation he had, here in the house, with a friend."

"Who was the friend?"

"Dr. Hardinxveld. He's a surgeon at St. Matthew's Hospital."

DeKok seemed baffled.

"And he discussed a fraud case with him?" There was confusion in his voice.

Mrs. Abbenes nodded with emphasis.

"I also heard, at that time, the name of the young man. They mentioned it several times."

"And what was that name?"

"Casper, Casper Hoogwoud."

DeKok wondered why he was not surprised.

Vledder's mouth fell open. He seemed bewildered as he looked at DeKok.

"Casper Hoogwoud involved in a bank fraud?"

DeKok nodded calmly.

"The case was being handled by the murdered attorney, Abbenes."

Vledder grinned, still in disbelief.

"In that case, the hundred thousand taped to his waist was not connected to some drug deal, as we assumed." He paused. "To tell you the truth, I had my doubts. After you left this morning I talked to narcotics. They've never heard the name Casper Hoogwoud."

"What about Marcel?"

"Oh, yes, they knew him, but only as a user, not as a dealer."

DeKok stared at his partner.

"Casper Hoogwoud," he said slowly, groping for a thought, "has a blank police record." He looked at the ceiling. "But are there any records that a court case, a law suit against him has been filed?"

"No."

DeKok shook his head.

"Then the injured bank has not filed an official complaint with the police."

"Why wouldn't they?"

DeKok waved nonchalantly.

"It happens sometimes...to avoid the publicity. Banks don't like to wash their dirty linen in public. It damages their reputation and the trust of their depositors."

"But I don't understand. How did Abbenes get involved? If no official complaint has been filed against Casper, how can Abbenes act as his attorney?"

DeKok raised a finger in the air.

"I don't think Abbenes was Casper's attorney, but he probably represented the bank as judicial advisor."

Vledder grinned.

"To see if they could contain the damage. Teflonize, as they call it in the U. S."

"That may have been their philosophy," nodded DeKok. "Make as little noise and get as much money back as possible."

"Are we required to inform the bank about Casper's hundred thousand?"

DeKok shook his head decisively.

"That's not our job, at least not for now. Officially we don't know anything. We don't even know which bank is involved."

"And how do we discover that?"

"Simple. We ask Casper," smiled DeKok.

"And if he won't talk?"

"I have one more arrow in my quiver."

"What?"

"Dr. Hardinxveld."

Vledder found a parking place close to where he had parked the night before. The area looked a lot better in the feeble sunlight than it had during the storm. The inspectors got out of the car and Vledder locked the vehicle.

"You remember where it is?" asked DeKok.

"Yes, just around the corner, number 876, downstairs. Just to make sure, I checked the log from last night."

DeKok nodded his approval.

"I wonder if we'll meet any sorrowing family members?"

"Perhaps the despotic father," offered Vledder.

"Indeed, the old-fashioned patriarch with outdated ideas about raising a family."

"You really think it's that bad?"

DeKok shrugged.

"As a young man I did not always see eye to eye with my father," he said nonchalantly. "Generations do collide."

They stopped in front of number 876 and DeKok gave a forceful tug on the pull bell. The result was an impressive noise.

"You'll wake the whole neighborhood," warned Vledder.

Casper opened the door within seconds. He wore the same trousers and blazer of the night before. With surprise he stared at the men on his doorstep.

"Are you returning my money already?" There was sarcasm in his voice.

DeKok shook his head.

"We just want to have a little chat."

"I thought we said everything there was to say yesterday?"

DeKok pretended not to hear.

"Is Marcel still in the house?"

The young man shook his head.

"No, the funeral home came to collect him early this morning. If Father or Marianne wants to see him, they'll have to go there. I don't want to spend another night under the same roof with a corpse."

It sounded hard and unfeeling. DeKok gave him a pensive look.

"I thought you liked your brother?"

Casper nodded unwillingly.

"Yes, *living* Marcel." He stopped and changed his tone of voice. "Let's go inside to continue this discussion. It doesn't have to be public entertainment."

He turned around and walked down the corridor. DeKok followed him as Vledder closed the door.

The living room looked onto a well-kept garden,

enclosed by a thick hedge of conifers. The high windows allowed a lot of light into the room, light that wasn't there the night before.

DeKok looked at the sofa where they had discovered Marcel's corpse. Then he looked at Casper. There was something in the young man's attitude that bothered him.

"Very early this morning," he began, "someone called us to say Marcel had been murdered."

Casper seemed genuinely surprised.

"Who called?"

"A woman…she didn't give her name."

The young man shrugged.

"An inappropriate joke."

DeKok remained unmoved.

"Was Marcel murdered?"

Casper raised both arms in a theatrical gesture of despair.

"Marcel died because of complications caused by AIDS," he said emotionally. "You were here…you heard what the doctor said. What else is there to talk about? Some kind of nut calls you and—" He did not complete the sentence. "When do I get my money back?"

DeKok's face remained calm, expressionless.

"That money is the result of fraud. You've swindled a bank."

Casper looked as if DeKok was from another planet.

"Who says so?"

"An attorney who says he represents the bank. J. O. B. Abbenes, Esquire."

The young man laughed a joyless short laugh.

"Abbenes, *Esquire*," he repeated with a mocking voice, "asked me to his office several times. He demanded I return

100,000 Euros. I am supposed to have swindled the Ijs-selstein Bank for that amount."

"And that is not so?"

Casper Hoogwoud grinned.

"Of course not. I have an account at the Ijsselstein Bank. Somebody deposited 100,000 in that account. I withdrew the money; all completely legal and above board. There was no fraud or swindle involved."

"Are you entitled to the money?"

"Apparently—apparently somebody wanted to please me."

DeKok snorted.

"Casper, your story reeks."

The young man reacted furiously.

"You know what reeks?" he cried sharply. "Abbenes is a big-time crook. The man threatened me with everything from the police to the underworld." He pointed an accusing finger at DeKok. "When you see him next, you can tell him he can forget about the money."

DeKok shook his head slowly.

"I won't tell him that. It would serve no purpose. Abbenes is dead."

Hoogwoud looked amazed. His mouth gaped open and his eyes widened. His hands began to shake.

"Dead?" he asked hoarsely.

DeKok nodded.

"Last night somebody bashed in his skull, resulting in an unpleasantly large hole."

"Who?"

DeKok looked at him, a faint smile on his face.

"You?"

5

Vledder drove aggressively away from the side of the
road. The much-abused engine of the old VW groaned
in protest. DeKok took a look at the door of 876 as they
passed. He was convinced it would not be the last time
he'd visit the premises.

The interview with young Casper Hoogwoud had been
unsatisfactory. It had given DeKok a nauseous feeling of
combined disappointment and unrest. There was clearly
something wrong with the young man; something sinister,
perhaps. Nobody deposits 100,000 Euros in the account of
an eighteen year old, just for the fun of it. He pushed his
old, felt hat down on his forehead and slid down in the seat.
Casper was a strong personality, who had shown a certain
mental flexibility and spiritual confidence. Even a direct
accusation of murder had left him undisturbed. That was
remarkable, especially in view of his age.

The old inspector scratched the back of his neck. There
had to be a way to penetrate the armor Casper had built
around himself. There had to be a weak spot, somewhere
the bastion could be breached.

Vledder broke into his thoughts.

"I never did get around to asking Dr. Rusteloos about
AIDS."

"Why not?"

"That man needs a hearing aid. It's almost impossible to have a normal conversation with him, especially while he's performing an autopsy. He speaks into a microphone to record his findings as he goes along."

"What about the wound?"

"It was immediately fatal."

"And the weapon?"

"That was rather difficult. The good doctor had never seen a head wound quite like that. There was no indication of a hammer, a handle, or even an axe."

DeKok sat upright.

"Was there any indication at all?"

"Blunt-force trauma was the cause of death. The shape of the weapon is indicated to be a kind of delta with a rounded point. Perhaps the best way to compare the shape of the wound is to that of a whale without a tail...I mean the curve on the back of the whale."

"Strange."

"Dr. Rusteloos agreed. Just to be on the safe side, we took some close ups. Bram Weelen promised to have the prints ready later today."

DeKok nodded his approval.

"What about the skull? Did Abbenes have a normal skull?"

"What do you mean?"

"Not very thin, a sort of 'egg-shell' skull?"

Vledder shook his head.

"The bone was of normal thickness. The blow to the head, with whatever weapon was used, must have been very forceful."

DeKok rubbed his nose with his little finger.

"Anything else of interest?"

The young inspector took a folded piece of tissue paper out of the breast pocket of his jacket and handed it to DeKok.

"When they undressed him, they found this around his neck."

DeKok unfolded the paper and looked at the item. It was a pendant of some sort, with a thin chain.

"It looks like a bull."

"That's right. *Taurus*, the bull. It's a constellation, and also a sign of the zodiac."

DeKok took the piece of jewelry in his hand. The bull was exquisitely modeled and from the weight he guessed it to be pure gold. It was rather heavy and he did not doubt it was also expensive.

"Everybody normally wears their astrological totem, don't they?"

Vledder smiled.

"Yes, yes, of course."

DeKok replaced the chain and the pendant back in the paper and folded it over. He placed it in Vledder's hand.

"There's something wrong."

"What?"

"The bull. Abbenes was born on the third of January. He was not a Taurus, rather a Capricorn."

Vledder parked the car behind the station house. They walked to Warmoes Street through Old Bridge Alley. Business was picking up in the quarter. DeKok lifted his hat to a smiling prostitute. She nodded in recognition. Only in Amsterdam could prostitutes practice their trade within half a block of a police station.

"What are we going to do with the pendant?"

"Keep it. We have other jewelry belonging to Abbenes. It's a good excuse for another visit to Mrs. Abbenes."

As they entered the lobby, Jan Kuster called them to the counter. He took a sheet out of the back of the log book and handed it to DeKok.

"Brandsma's report."

"Who is Brandsma?"

"The constable you asked to check the hoods of the cars along the canal, remember?"

"Oh, yes," answered DeKok. "And?"

Jan Kuster pointed at the report.

"Just read it. There was only one car with a warm hood in the neighborhood, a gray Mercedes. Brandsma also tracked the tag number. The car is registered to a Dr. D. E. L. Hardinxveld."

DeKok wrinkled his nose, as if he had smelled something foul.

"Hardinxveld?" he repeated.

Kuster nodded.

"A surgeon at St. Matthew's Hospital."

DeKok sank down in the chair behind his desk. He was just about to toss Constable Brandsma's report in a drawer when Vledder intervened.

"Hey, hey," he protested. "Give me that. I want to enter it in the computer. We don't have too much, so far. At least it will flesh out what we have. It will keep the commissaris happy."

"Oh, very well," grumbled DeKok. "But I suspect it will keep you even happier. You know, Dick," he continued pontifically, "I have noticed a tendency toward bureaucracy in you. You must fight that, my boy. It may lead to a promotion."

Vledder grinned.

"Well, it is a good report, and it may help us."

"Yes, that it is," admitted DeKok. "A good report, I mean. I don't know yet whether it will help us."

"But it's possible."

"What?"

"Abbenes could have driven Hardinxveld's car. His wife told you they were friends."

"But I think it likely that Abbenes had a car of his own."

"Probably broken down in a garage, somewhere," guessed Vledder.

DeKok shook his head in disagreement.

"People like that immediately get a loaner from their garage. Most are insured for the expense."

Vledder looked away from his screen.

"Still, you think it might mean something after all?"

DeKok nodded slowly.

"I'm not certain. But you are right that Dr. Hardinxveld has some explaining to do," he offered somberly.

A man appeared in the doorway of the detective room. He talked to the detective nearest the door. After a brief conversation, the officer pointed in the direction of DeKok's desk. The visitor made his way through the crowded detective room. DeKok observed him. The man was about fifty years old and wore a baggy gray suit. The elbows and knees were shiny with age. He stopped in front of DeKok's desk.

"You're Inspector DeKok?"

The gray sleuth looked up at the man.

"With a kay-oh-kay," he answered.

"I had expected you at our office," said the man, disapproval in his voice.

"And what office might that be?" asked DeKok.

"The Abbenes law office, of course. My name is Dungen, Charles Dungen. I'm the clerk, or rather, the right-hand man of Mr. Abbenes." He gave DeKok a sad look. "After the terrible happenings of last night.... I waited all morning for you."

Vledder made an entry on the keyboard and then stood up. With a polite gesture he offered the man a chair. Dungen pushed the chair a little closer to DeKok's desk. His face had a sallow, jaundiced tint. He looked tense.

"Perhaps I can give you some valuable information," said Dungen, nervously. "I have enjoyed the complete trust and confidence of Mr. Abbenes for years. I am *au courant* regarding all his cases."

DeKok leaned closer.

"Including those cases," he asked with a smirk, "that could not stand the light of day?"

Dungen showed himself to be highly indignant.

"That remark was gratuitous, Inspector," he said severely. "I'm personally offended. You should be aware that Mr. Abbenes was an attorney with high ethical standards. He did not take any questionable cases. He would *never* have involved himself in cases that are less, eh, that could not stand the light of day. His conduct was beyond reproach."

DeKok gave him a winning smile.

"I respect your feelings," he said sweetly. "From your remarks I conclude that you were very much attached to your employer."

Charles Dungen nodded in agreement.

"Absolutely. And I have every reason for that. I have worked beside him very pleasantly for almost twenty years." He paused and looked at Vledder. Then he returned his attention to DeKok. "His sudden, eh, demise, however, makes my future a bit uncertain. Although I presume that his successor will keep me in his employ." He tapped the side of his head with an index finger. "There's a lot of practical knowledge up here."

"Is it known who his successor is to be?"

"No."

"Mr. Abbenes had no partners, no associates?"

Dungen shook his head.

"Mr. Abbenes was an individualist, a man who found it difficult to delegate."

DeKok nodded his understanding.

"Did you have any difficulty with that?"

"Sometimes. I was always ready to lighten his load, so to speak, to relieve some of the burden. But he did not always allow that."

"Do you know Mrs. Abbenes?"

Dungen's face fell.

"His married life was not exactly, eh, fortuitous," he said sadly. "I mean, the marriage did not bring him the happiness he might have expected from such a relationship."

DeKok smiled. He was amused by the way Dungen expressed himself.

"Did he compensate?"

Dungen seemed confused.

"What? Compensate for an unhappy marriage?" he asked hesitantly.

"Exactly. Friends, other women?"

Charles Dungen made a vague gesture. The question obviously embarrassed him.

"Mr. Abbenes," he said carefully, "spent a lot of time at the clubhouse."

"He was a member of a club?"

"The golf club, Amstel Land. If I needed him urgently, I could often reach him there. That is also where he met his friends."

"Dr. Hardinxveld?"

Dungen nodded calmly.

"I've also met him at the office—Don Hardinxveld, surgeon at St. Matthew's."

"Do you know any other friends...women friends?"

Dungen shrugged.

"I know nothing about girlfriends," he said testily. "He met other friends at the club besides Dr. Hardinxveld. But I don't know those people. Mr. Abbenes kept his private life separate from the office environment, as much as possible."

DeKok glanced at Vledder, who was unobtrusively making notes.

"You have never noticed anything about relationships with women?" he asked with incredulity. "Mr. Abbenes was a handsome, wealthy man, who did not receive tenderness from his legal spouse. I would have thought that..." He did not complete the thought, but gave his visitor a penetrating look. "You must have heard conversations with women in the office."

Charles Dungen moved in his chair, as if to distance himself from DeKok.

"Those conversations always concerned business, legal business."

DeKok leaned back and scratched the back of his neck.

A feeling of self-pity overcame him. Here he was, he thought, beating his brains out over yet one more murder case. With an effort he banished the depressing thought and produced a wan smile.

"Didn't you say you might have some useful information?"

Dungen nodded with emphasis.

"I know who killed Mr. Abbenes."

"Who?" DeKok asked evenly.

With precise movements Charles Dungen took a notebook from an inside pocket and opened it.

"Franciscus," he said primly. "Franciscus Kraay, File Number PLX 84."

6

"Franciscus Kraay?"

Charles Dungen again nodded with emphasis.

"He is a client; a wild, somewhat primitive man. He has a violent, explosive temper."

"And this Kraay murdered Mr. Abbenes?"

"I'm convinced of it."

"And what makes you so convinced?"

Dungen moved in his chair, closer to DeKok's desk.

"Early this year Mr. Abbenes represented Kraay in a divorce proceeding. Kraay was displeased with the final conditions of the settlement. In fact, he completely disagreed. The alimony was too high, in his opinion. He held Mr. Abbenes responsible for the judgment. He suggested, said right out, Mr. Abbenes had been influenced by his attractive ex-wife."

DeKok smiled.

"I presume," he said calmly, "emotions are often in an uproar in divorce proceedings. Would you say such accusations happen more often than not?"

"Certainly. Sometimes the wild theatricals occur in our office. It cannot always be avoided. But there is seldom any physical violence."

"But there was with Kraay?"

Charles Dungen gestured impatiently.

"I told you, the man is violent, reacts at the most primitive level. He's as strong as an ox. He knocked me to the ground with a single movement of his arm when I did not admit him to Mr. Abbenes' private office. It was also the first time he voiced deadly threats."

DeKok leaned his head to one side.

"Deadly threats?" he repeated skeptically.

The tone did not escape Dungen. He looked up briefly and then consulted his notebook.

"Kraay actually said, 'Believe me, my man, I'll bash your head in.' He repeated that threat at least three other times. I have noted the times when he spoke those words, together with dates and places."

"Why?"

"What do you mean?"

DeKok spread his arms wide.

"Why did you keep such an accurate record?"

Dungen shook his head.

"I have the feeling," he said chidingly, "you do not appreciate my statements as you should. You do not realize what kind of man Kraay is." He raised his hands in a gesture of despair. "These were not meaningless threats of a powerless man who angrily relieved his feelings. On the contrary Kraay meant every word he said. His words were calm and precise; he said them without feeling. Both Mr. Abbenes and I took him seriously. In view of our past experiences with Mr. Kraay, we did not think even for a moment that he would *not* fulfill his threats. We remained vigilant." He paused, lowered his head and continued in a somber tone, "This morning when I learned Mr. Abbenes had been killed on his own doorstep with a blow to the head, Kraay came to mind as the perpetrator. I was convinced, especially since time was running out for the next installment."

"What time was running out, what installment?"

Dungen sighed and explained.

"Last night, midnight, was the time limit Kraay had given Mr. Abbenes. If Mr. Abbenes had not negotiated different terms for his divorce by the deadline, Kraay would irrevocably proceed to the next installment of the drama. He would execute his threats.

"Are we going to arrest him?"

"Who?" asked DeKok.

"Franciscus Kraay, of course," said Vledder, irritated.

DeKok shrugged.

"First I want to know more."

"More?" asked Vledder mockingly. "It's very clear to me. The man threatened to bash in Abbenes' skull—"

DeKok interrupted.

"There is a dent in his skull."

"Precisely," agreed Vledder. "Think about the time limit...the next installment to begin at midnight. It cannot be coincidence Abbenes' killer struck a few hours after the deadline."

"It is indeed remarkable," said DeKok calmly.

Vledder gave his older colleague a searching look. His face was serious.

"And I have to say you treated Dungen rather shabbily. That man was genuinely interested in helping us. But most of the time it seemed like you did not really believe him."

DeKok leaned back in his chair.

"I'll confess something to you," he said slowly. "I know

Frankie Kraay. They used to call him "The Crow." I had something to do with him a long time ago."

"How long ago?"

"Oh, about fifteen years back, maybe longer. He lived on a quiet stretch of Gelder Canal. In those days, The Crow was always ready to do something if he thought some kind of injustice had been done."

"Violently?"

"Usually."

"Primitive?"

"As a rule."

Vledder leaned forward.

"So, what else do you want?" He could not control the irritation in his voice. "Everything comes together very nicely. This time, according to him, the injustice had been committed against *him*." He paused and thought for a moment. "And then think of the phone call we received: 'Not according to your righteousness, but mine.' That seems clearly in character for Kraay."

DeKok gave his agitated colleague a long, considering look.

"Only one problem, Dick. A woman made the phone call."

DeKok suddenly realized the car had not moved for awhile. He pressed himself up in the seat and saw the long row of cars on the Damrak waiting for the traffic lights. Most were headed for Dam Square.

"I thought we would have been much farther along," he murmured to himself. "What time is it?" he asked Vledder.

Vledder pointed at the clock on the dashboard.

"Just about a quarter to four," he said patiently. He knew DeKok had a watch somewhere. But it was one of those old-fashioned chain watches. DeKok never consulted it. Of course a wristwatch would be too modern, thought Vledder, not for the first time.

"Well," said DeKok, "if this keeps up much longer, we'll be too late."

Vledder shrugged.

"What can you expect? It's the beginning of rush hour. It will only get worse." He paused while he moved the car about three feet. "Does it have to be today?"

"Never put off till tomorrow what can be done today," said DeKok.

Vledder grinned.

"Another saying from your old mother?"

"You're starting to get to know my family."

They progressed another few feet.

"What do you hope to achieve at the Ijsselstein Bank?"

DeKok gestured vaguely.

"Mr. Darthouse, the managing director, is prepared to receive us. That's quite an achievement in itself."

"But not an answer to my question," noted Vledder.

DeKok rubbed his nose with his little finger.

"I still can't get out of my mind the 100,000 Euros that Casper carried taped to his waist. It bothers me. Perhaps we can get a look at Casper's bank account."

"And then what?"

DeKok grinned wickedly.

"Call it official curiosity. It intrigues me why someone would handle that kind of money so carelessly."

"You want to know *who* deposited that money into his account."

DeKok nodded.

"And why. I'm rather suspicious when it comes to grand gestures."

They crawled along in silence. The traffic became denser, as Vledder had predicted. DeKok looked at the dashboard clock. Darthouse promised to wait until four thirty—it was now almost twenty-five minutes past the hour. Time was pressing.

Vledder cursed at the driver in front of him.

"Did you tell Darthouse why you wanted to talk to him?" he asked, as the car in front suddenly turned out of the way.

"I had no choice. Darthouse wanted to prepare himself and gather whatever information he needed. I can understand. I remained as vague as possible, but I could not avoid mentioning Casper Hoogwoud's name. I would have preferred to see him unprepared...using the element of surprise, so to speak."

Vledder finally turned onto Emperors Canal.

"You know, DeKok, there's something I don't understand."

"What?"

"Why didn't you mention Casper Hoogwoud when you were talking to Dungen? Perhaps he could have given you some useful information."

DeKok turned toward his colleague.

"I thought about it, Dick. But I decided against it very early in the conversation. You see, Charles Dungen is one of two things; he's either extremely naïve, or he purposely presents a false image of an ethical Abbenes. Either way, I thought it more prudent not to mention Casper Hoogwoud and his questionable 100,000 Euros." He waved

nonchalantly. "Never fear. I'm not through with our dedicated Charles Dungen...not by a long shot."

Vledder found a narrow spot between the trees. DeKok
had to get out of the car before he pulled in. Even so, there
was barely room enough to allow Vledder to get out. When
he finally wriggled from behind the steering wheel, DeKok
asked him for the time. Vledder looked at his watch.

"He may be gone, DeKok, we're almost twelve minutes
late."

DeKok curled his lips in disappointment.

"Let's hope," he said piously, "justice is worth an extra
twelve minutes to Mr. Darthouse."

Vledder nodded and started to cross the street.

After climbing the imposing stairs, they entered the lobby
and walked to an information booth. A man in a neat, dark-
blue uniform with silver lapels waited for them expectantly.

DeKok lifted his hat slightly.

We're police inspectors—Vledder and DeKok, Warmoes
Street. We have an appointment with Mr. Darthouse."

The man looked up at an enormous clock on the marble
wall. Then he looked down at the inspectors.

"By this time of day," he said severely, "Mr. Darthouse
is no longer in the building."

DeKok made an apologetic gesture.

"I'm sorry. We were delayed by traffic. But Mr. Darthouse promised to wait for us."

With obvious reluctance, the man left the booth and
disappeared through a high door in the back of the lobby.
He returned a few minutes later and led the inspectors to
an elevator.

"Second floor," he said. "Mr. Darthouse's secretary is waiting for you."

DeKok again lifted his hat in thanks. When the elevator doors opened on the second floor, they found an attractive woman in a severe business suit waiting for them. She smiled professionally.

"If you gentlemen will follow me?" she invited.

Vledder and DeKok followed her through a wide corridor of pink marble. At the end she lifted the ornate handle of a heavy, carved door. She made an inviting gesture and departed without a sound.

Mr. Darthouse turned out to be a tall, stately man with a tanned face and straight, blonde hair. He was seated in a large chair with a high back, behind an ornate, oaken desk. He waived at a couple of chairs in front of the desk without getting up.

"Please have a seat," he said. "How may I be of assistance?"

It did not sound unfriendly.

DeKok placed his old, dilapidated hat on the floor next to the chair. Then he looked at their host.

"We have the sad task," he said soberly, "to investigate the untimely, violent passing of Mr. Abbenes, Esquire. He had an office on this same canal."

Darthouse nodded.

"I heard about it and, I must say, the event shocked me. I knew Mr. Abbenes very well. We were, how shall I put it, we were friends." He paused and stared at the inspectors. "Therefore I am more than willing to help you in your investigation in any way within in my power."

DeKok nodded gratefully.

"Our investigations have not yielded much result in

the short time that has gone by. But we understand Mr. Abbenes had a large practice."

Darthouse smiled.

"That is common knowledge. Mr. Abbenes was an extremely competent attorney."

"We are not excluding the possibility," continued DeKok, "that the motive for the murder may be found in one of the cases in which Mr. Abbenes was involved."

Darthouse nodded his agreement.

"Indeed a reasonable assumption."

DeKok rubbed the bridge of his nose with his little finger.

"We have learned," he said carefully, "that Mr. Abbenes was working on a case involving a young man, Casper Hoogwoud. I mentioned the name over the telephone. Mr. Hoogwoud allegedly swindled your bank out of 100,000 Euros."

With a slow movement, Mr. Darthouse brought both hands together and placed the tips of his fingers against each other.

"I don't know," he said icily, "the source of this so-called information, but Mr. Abbenes was not handling a case like that because we have not been swindled."

DeKok widened his eyes.

"Have you any information on Casper Hoogwoud?"

"He is not known to us."

DeKok swallowed his disappointment.

"He did, however, have an account here."

Darthouse shook his head calmly.

"Nobody by that name has ever had an account in this bank."

7

Inspector DeKok left the Ijsselstein Bank with an intense feeling of dejection. He knew the managing director had lied to him and there was probably no hope in penetrating those lies. He could hardly turn the entire bank administration topsy-turvy. Still he considered the possibilities, only to admit that all his brainstorming was futile.

Vledder seemed more cheerful. The young inspector appeared to be filled with happy thoughts. The visit to the bank had not depressed him. On the contrary he gave the impression Darthouse's remarks had revived him.

After a bit of maneuvering, Vledder freed the car from its narrow space, enabling DeKok to get in as well. Once on the quay along the canal, there was suddenly no easy way to proceed. The canal sides and the side streets were clogged with vehicles.

After several tries, amid the angry horn signals of other vehicles, DeKok made a dismissive gesture with his hands.

"Just find a place to wait," he said resignedly. "Sooner or later we'll be able to move."

Vledder acted surprised.

"Do you want to spend the night here?"

DeKok's face, which normally looked like that of a good-natured boxer, was sad.

"He sounded bleak. I think we're better off doing

nothing," he said. "We need to just stop, give it up. I have the feeling every step we've taken in this case has been the wrong one."

Vledder put the car half on the roadway and half on the sidewalk. He turned on his hazard lights and shut off the engine.

"That's nonsense, and you know it," he rebutted, shaking his head. "Or is it because Darthouse told us that Hoogwoud never had an account with that bank? That only means Casper lied. Casper cannot tell us the true source of that money without compromising himself. That's why he spins a different tale every time we talk. First he says he won it gambling, next it was an unknown benefactor who deposited the money in his account." He grinned. "Lies, all lies."

DeKok looked pensive.

"There's more to the money than is apparent. We're missing a thread somewhere, a connection." He paused and pulled his lower lip out. Then he let it plop back. It was a disgusting sight and always annoyed Vledder.

"All right," said Vledder, more to stop DeKok from doing what he was doing than to elicit an answer. "Where's the thread?"

"For one thing Mrs. Abbenes must have known about hundreds of cases her husband handled. Why would she specifically remember the Casper Hoogwoud incident? And why would Darthouse say with such conviction he had never heard of Hoogwoud? Why deny there was any such case?"

Vledder did not answer. He shrugged and looked at his partner's sad face.

"Do you have tired feet?" he asked, suddenly concerned.

DeKok laughed heartily. He understood Vledder's question. Usually when a case appeared hopeless, when he saw no immediate solution, his legs would act up. He had been assured more than once it was purely psychosomatic, but the pain was almost unbearable even so. He always referred to it as "tired feet." Still laughing, he shook his head.

"Not yet," he said with a chuckle. "No protest from my little devils with red-hot pitchforks. But if something doesn't change quickly—" He did not get the opportunity to complete his sentence. Vledder spotted a small opening in the traffic. With one movement he started the car and slammed it into reverse. He made a hair-raising, sliding turn and shot into a narrow alley.

"I have a wonderful idea," exclaimed Vledder as they raced down the alley.

"Well?"

"You're going to Little Lowee. I am certain that the taste of a good cognac will lift you out of your misery. I'll drop you off."

DeKok smiled.

"Dick," he said, "you should have been a prophet."

With the smile still on his face he slid down in the seat. His despair was rapidly driven away by hopeful thoughts.

The dimly lit, intimate bar was near the corner of Barn Alley. Little Lowee, the proprietor, peered from behind the bar as DeKok hoisted himself onto a bar stool and looked around. It was his usual spot at the end of the bar, his back to the wall with a clear view of the rest of the establishment. Lowee's was not busy—too early for the usual crowd of prostitutes and other underworld figures. He waved casually at two aging prostitutes who were drinking coffee.

He placed his old hat on his knee and relaxed against the wall. It was one of his favorite watering holes. Whenever he and Vledder could spare the time, they would stop by and be greeted by the diminutive barkeep.

Little Lowee had watched him get settled and now spoke for the first time. His mousey face beamed with good will.

"Good to see ya, DeKok," he said in his almost incomprehensible thieves language. "Bin too long, awready." He looked past DeKok. "So, where's your side kick, ennyway?"

"Yes, it has," answered DeKok, "it must have been almost a week since I last enjoyed your special cognac." He added, "Vledder wanted to finish some paperwork at the office, he didn't feel like a drink."

"Is dadda hint?" asked Lowee, diving under the bar and emerging with a venerable, dusty bottle. "I'm gonna take care o' that."

He produced two large snifters and, with infinite care, uncorked the bottle. With a practiced movement he filled the glasses, then replaced the bottle on the bar. He pushed one glass in DeKok's direction and lifted the other one.

DeKok picked up the glass and leisurely absorbed the aroma of the golden liquid while he warmed the glass in his hand. After a few minutes he took his first, savoring sip. He rolled the liquid around in his mouth and, with an indescribable sense of wellbeing, felt it trickle down his gullet.

Lowee had copied his movements and for awhile the two men remained silent in admiration and appreciation of the remarkable drink. Then Lowee replaced his glass on the bar.

"Yo bin busy, then? Like I says, ain't seen youse for awhile."

DeKok smiled.

"Somewhat," he said, taking a larger sip. "You know, Lowee, I almost forgot the taste. Where *do* you get these bottles?"

"I got me sources," said Lowee secretively.

DeKok nodded.

"Well, whatever your sources, I hope they'll be able to supply you for a longtime."

"Don't worry, they ain't gonna let me run dry."

"Good," said DeKok and drained his glass.

As Lowee came closer to refill it, DeKok leaned toward him.

"Hear anything about The Crow lately?"

Lowee's face fell and became sad.

"You want 'im or what?"

DeKok smiled soothingly.

"Worried, Lowee?"

The small barkeep shrugged his narrow shoulders.

"Well, I gotta a soft spot for da Crow."

DeKok nodded agreement.

"Me, too."

"But you wanna grabbem, anyhow?"

DeKok made an apologetic gesture.

"What do you want?" he said resignedly. "I can't have him bashing in the heads of lawyers."

"Ah, Abbenes, right? He done that?"

DeKok rubbed his chin.

"What do you think, Lowee?"

He stared for a long time into the distance without saying anything. His face was serious.

"Ya knows, DeKok," he said finally, "when I read it in da swindle sheets, I thinks da_Crow done it awright." He tapped his chest. "But deep inside I think it ain't possible, just can't believe it, *kneisie?*"

"Why not?" asked DeKok, reflecting that if Vledder had been with him he would have had to explain that "kneisie," with the *k* clearly pronounced, meant "you know" in Lowee's underworld language of Bargoens.

Lowee drained his glass in turn.

"Da Crow gotta a big mouth, as big as the Queen's garage." He held up his right hand with his thumb and index finger just a centimeter apart. "But 'e's gotta heart the size of a peanut."

DeKok's face became stubborn.

"In the old days he was always ready with his fists."

"Ach, he was young, just showin' off."

DeKok smiled.

"Has he been here since Abbenes' murder?"

"Nope."

"Heard from him?"

"Nope."

"On the lam?"

Little Lowee shook his head.

"You muzzent look at it dat way." He paused and refilled his glass. "You see," he continued in a didactic tone of voice, "Da Crow blabs all'a time 'e's gonna whack da mouthpiece. Word onn'a street gotta be he done it. An' da Crow knows dat."

"I see," said DeKok. "Why did he dislike that lawyer?"

Lowee filled his glass again and took a sip before he answered.

"Da Crow," he said, "da Crow ain't had it easy. He blew

the quarter ten years ago. His fame got inna way, ya know. Everybody here knows he's good wid 'is hands, but don't think aboudit. First he goes off, then, bam! Somebody gonna get hit. He don' have a future, just a rep."

"That's why I lost track of him."

Lowee nodded, as if he were proud of DeKok's understanding.

"He still gotta mother in the neighborhood. She stops by now an'en. Tha's how come I know da Crow gone to Utrecht. He gotta a store there—bikes, widda engine, or not, you know, both kinds. He knows all aboudit. He done well wid' some moollah from an uncle, got big." Lowee replaced his glass and his face fell again. "Then, two years ago he meets da broad."

"What kind of woman?"

"She's called Sophie," grinned Lowee. "Good lookin' broad, maybe not a hunnert percent, but with everything and all in da right places, ya knows. An' da Crow was a goner inna flash. Inna month they was hitched. And that's when all hell broke loose." Lowee shrugged. "Not all atta same time."

"What kind of trouble?"

"Well, Sophie cheated Crow from the start. At first da Crow wooden hear of it. Thinks people rat on her to pester 'im, ya know. Then one day 'e comes home and finds 'er in bed wiv anudder guy. He throws 'er in the street and gets 'isself a mouthpiece."

"Abbenes."

"Yep."

"To get a divorce?"

Little Lowee nodded slowly.

"Exacto…and learned da hard way." He spread both arms.

"Wadda broad done wiv da mouthpiece, I dunno—not my binniz. But she musta thrown 'er body inna ring. So what 'appens? Dat mouthpiece fixes a joke agreement. Da Crow looses it all...everything he worked for."

"That bad?"

"Sure. Da boy is broke. He might as well sell da binniz in Utrecht."

DeKok looked thoughtful.

"But Frankie doesn't have to agree to the arrangements the lawyer made. He can appeal to the courts."

Lowee gave him a pitying look.

"Wadda ya think a guy as da Crow knows about da courts? That Abbenes was a good mouthpiece, specialized in divorces." He sighed. "An' da Crow thinks he's okay, she done *him* wrong by sleeping around."

DeKok listened and rubbed his chin.

"What is more serious is that Frankie uttered some stupid threats in Abbenes' office, in front of witnesses."

Lowee closed his eyes.

"Wadda sad sack." He meant every word.

DeKok took another sip and immediately replaced the glass on the counter. He could no longer enjoy the cognac. He looked at Lowee.

"Could Frankie have done it, after all?"

Lowee reacted surprised.

"You da cop, or Lowee da cop?"

Silently DeKok slid off the bar stool and replaced his hat on his head.

Little Lowee pointed at DeKok's glass, which still showed a generous measure of cognac in the bottom.

"You gonna finish it?"

"No."

"I unnerstand," said Lowee. He emptied the glass in the sink and put it in the wash sink. "I'm all tore to pieces about it, too. Ain't no picnic for Martha, either."

"Who is Martha?"

Lowee smiled tenderly.

"Nice little broad, she's a bit stiff, *kneisie*. Da Crow brung 'er here once. Since Sophie gone orf, 'e's sorta sweet on Martha." He shook his head, grinning. "You gonna say not da Crow's cup o' tea. But he's taken widd 'er. Itsa sorta prim little thing...a broad from the black stockin' church, ya knows, always yakking about God, love, and eternal justice."

DeKok's eyes widened.

"Justice," he repeated, savoring the word on his tongue.

8

DeKok aimed his old hat at the peg on the wall and then stopped in surprise. He had actually managed to hit the peg and his hat stayed on it, gently swinging. It happened once every two years, at most. He recovered quickly, as if nothing extraordinary had happened. He stripped off his raincoat and walked slowly toward his desk. But there was a triumphant gleam in his eyes.

Vledder stood up from behind his desk, where he'd been fastidiously updating information into his computer, looked up at the large clock on the wall, and then planted himself in front of DeKok's desk. It was a quarter past eight.

"May I remind you we haven't eaten yet." There was a gentle rebuke in his voice.

DeKok nodded vaguely.

"Why don't you go downstairs and see if there's anyone who can fix us some ham and eggs."

Recently, the old police station had added a kitchen, like a fire station. The shortage of personnel necessitated longer work hours for the officers on duty. The city responded by making sure they would not have to go home to eat or stop by some restaurant to take valuable time away from their duties. The system worked haphazardly because no regular cook was assigned. The various officers took turns, schedules permitting.

"And if there's nobody there?"

"Then do it yourself."

"You don't want to go home?"

"No."

Vledder shook his head in disapproval.

"Yesterday I pulled another late night. I need my bed."

DeKok ignored the remark and his hungry stomach.
Instead he filled Vledder in on his conversation with
Lowee.

"Why don't you call the police in Utrecht?" DeKok offered.
"Perhaps they know where Frankie Kraay can be found.
He'll probably feel safer there than in Amsterdam." He
paused to rub his chin. "I'm also interested in his new
girlfriend, Martha. But she will probably be more difficult
to track down."

Vledder leaned back in his chair.

"It seems the outlook for The Crow is not hopeful. You
may have a soft spot for the man," he added mockingly,
"but to me he's the ideal suspect." Making a grand gesture
with his arm, he added, "And we've got it documented he
threatened Abbenes."

"If all threats resulted in real murders, then you would
never have time to eat or sleep," said DeKok.

Vledder reacted sharply.

"Abbenes is dead. So the threat didn't stay just a threat."
He looked up and changed his tone of voice. "Besides, you,
yourself, are not sure that The Crow is innocent."

DeKok looked surprised.

"And where do you get that idea?"

Vledder snorted.

"I know you, DeKok. How long have we been working together? I can just imagine the way you reacted when Little Lowee used the word *justice*. You immediately thought about *righteousness*. I can see it all as if I had been there."

The old sleuth lowered his head somewhat.

"You're right, Dick," he admitted. The moment Lowee said something about Martha, I immediately thought about the woman who called our commissaris after Abbenes' murder."

Vledder quoted, with an even tone, "Not because of your righteousness, but because of mine."

DeKok put down his knife and fork and took another sip of coffee. He looked at his partner with new appreciation.

"You fixed this yourself?"

Vledder nodded.

"Everybody was gone."

"Well, it's excellent. The toast is just right, the ham is just the right shade of brown, and the eggs are perfection, not easy with sunny-side up. My compliments."

The young inspector stood up, gathered the plates and cutlery, and stacked them on a nearby desk.

"It's one of only two dishes I cook," he grinned. "This is the only one that always works."

The detective room was nearly deserted when someone knocked on the door. Vledder called "Enter," but nothing happened. Through the frosted glass they could see the light in the hall outline a shadow. The figure wore a cape with a hood, reminiscent, thought DeKok, of Little Red Riding Hood.

"Come in," yelled Vledder, louder, as he hastily transferred the used plates to the floor under the desk.

The door opened slowly. A young woman appeared in the door opening. DeKok looked at her. He estimated her age at between twenty-five and thirty, probably closer to thirty. She was beautiful, very beautiful. Not fragile, but tall and slender. She looked as though she would be well able to take care of herself, the type of woman DeKok admired. She threw the rain hood back. Long, blonde hair came down in waves to her blue-purple cape. She unhooked the cape and removed the garment with an elegant gesture from her shoulders. A carpet of tiny raindrops colored the floor.

Vledder hastened closer and took the cape from her. She looked at him for a moment and gave him a wan smile. Then she undulated in the direction of DeKok. The gray sleuth rose with alacrity. He made a slight bow and courteously offered her a chair.

"Please be seated," he said.

"Thank you very much."

There was a soft, dark timbre to her voice. She sat down, placed her purse on the edge of the desk, and crossed her shapely legs. DeKok's glance passed over her knees. She wore thick, black stockings and her shoes were flat, sturdy walking shoes.

He sank down in the chair behind his desk.

"My name is DeKok," he said winningly, "with a kay-oh-kay." He waved in the direction of Vledder, who had hung her cape on a peg and walked closer. "This is Inspector Vledder." A playful smile spread across his face. "How may we be of service?"

Her face became pensive; she was apparently looking for a way to start the conversation.

"Perhaps," she said softly, "if I introduce myself first.

My name is Marianne...Marianne Hoogwoud, the sister of
Casper and Marcel."

DeKok leaned forward.

"In that case allow me to express my sympathy for the
untimely death of your brother Marcel," he said formally.

Marianne pressed the outstretched hand.

"Thank you."

The gray sleuth leaned back with a sigh.

"AIDS," he said sadly, "is a terrible disease."

Marianne nodded to herself.

"And still no cure," she said with anguish. "The virus
attacks just those organs that could produce the antidotes,
such as the liver and the lymph glands. That is what
causes the loss of immunity. Other microorganisms, normally destroyed by the body's natural defenses, reproduce
unchecked. Did you know AIDS patients usually die of
diseases normally kept in check by the antibodies we produce?" Her face was distorted by a caustic smile. "Did you
know it resembles swine fever?"

DeKok looked startled.

"Swine fever?" he repeated.

Marianne Hoogwoud nodded vehemently. It was as if
something disturbed her. Red spots appeared in her neck.
After a slight pause she said, "I have to confess something."
Her lips quavered and her voice sounded unsteady. "I regret
it, I'm sorry."

"What about?"

She worried nervously with the collar of her blouse.

"When Casper called me that night, to tell me that
Marcel had died of AIDS, I was not just sad, i* was so angry.
It is very difficult to accept Marcel's death. I feel *everybody*,
the entire medical profession, is guilty of his death." She

looked at DeKok. "In these modern times a plague like this should have no place."

The old man did not answer. For several seconds he expressionlessly observed her face closely.

"What about your confession?" His voice was insistent.

Marianne lowered her eyes a little.

"I called you that night and said that Marcel had been murdered."

"That was you?"

"Yes."

DeKok made a vague gesture in her direction.

"But you did not mean it literally."

She shook her head.

"It was an impulse, really, an act of pure impotence. I felt at the time Marcel had been murdered." She raised her hands above her head. "I do not blame or hold any particular individual responsible. My brother was failed by civilization, by a social order in which the health of the community is not a priority."

DeKok listened carefully to her tone and sentence structure.

"Is that why you did not use a name?" He rubbed his nose with his little finger.

Marianne Hoogwoud sighed deeply.

"You mustn't blame me. At the very moment I contacted you, I realized I was talking to the wrong person, the wrong office. The police were not involved in Marcel's death...it was not even a police matter. I realized I had not thought it through. My childish reaction was an automatic response, unthinking and impulsive. To make sure you would not mistakenly pursue an investigation, I decided to come here and identify myself."

"Courageous."

A sad smile played around her lips.

"A person should be prepared to face up to her decisions. I am willing to accept the consequences of my acts."

DeKok nodded agreement.

"Did your...eh, your father help you to come to that conclusion?"

"Father agreed I should do it. He's very much upset by Marcel's death. Marcel was the apple of his eye. He always hoped that Marcel would go further than he had, become something more than a golf club greenskeeper."

DeKok reacted with an uncertain gesture.

"Casper told us your father is a greenskeeper. He's the person who takes care of the golf courses, particularly the putting greens?"

Marianne smiled.

"Yes, but that's a rather simple explanation. Father has dozens of other responsibilities."

"Even so, it seems a rather lonesome profession."

Marianne nodded in agreement.

"We always enjoyed living there, on the Amstel Land property. Father is highly regarded by both the members and the directors of the club...with justification, I think." She took a deep breath. "But Father had expected more from Marcel. Marcel had a good head, but refused to use his intelligence for a worthwhile goal. He had no interest in an ordinary job. He said he wanted to get rich quickly and, much to my father's sorrow, left home at an early age."

"How?"

"What do you mean?"

"How did Marcel intend to get rich quickly?"

"Women don't have that urge as much, I think," said

Marianne with a somber smile. "But men always seem to be in search of some sort of blue print for wealth and success."

DeKok rubbed his chin and felt the stubble. It had been a long time since he last shaved.

"Is there such a blue print?" he asked naively.

She did not answer at once. She placed both hands in her lap and searched for an appropriate answer.

"When I saw...eh," she began hesitantly, "Marcel's lifestyle, his wealth, I sometimes had the feeling Marcel *had* found the right blue print."

"Did you know what he did?"

She shook her head.

"I don't think anyone knew what Marcel did."

"Not even a suspicion?"

"No."

"How did your father react to Marcel's apparent wealth?"

She shrugged.

"Sometimes it seemed he was actually proud of Marcel. But Father has changed in recent years. His mind is still strong, but physically he's breaking down fast. We've already brought his bed downstairs. One leg is stiff from the hip down, so he cannot manage the stairs anymore. I'm afraid Marcel's early death will only worsen his physical condition."

The gray sleuth nodded his understanding. Then he gave her a sharp look.

"Do you think Casper has taken over the so-called blue print, during Marcel's illness?"

Marianne Hoogwoud looked at him without fear.

"Casper," she said harshly, "is a child."

DeKok grinned.

"He seems rather precocious for an eighteen year old."

She narrowed her mouth and shook her head.

"It's all just a game to Casper...he's posing. His behavior has nothing to do with adulthood. As an old, experienced inspector, you should be able to see that." It sounded like an accusation.

DeKok did not react.

"When we arrested him," he said patiently, "he had 100,000 Euros taped to his waist. We still don't know the origin of the money."

"I know the story," shrugged Marianne. "I don't know where the money came from." She gave him a baleful look. "Nor am I interested."

DeKok sighed. He felt further insistence would be a waste of time. Marianne Hoogwoud did not look like the sort of woman who would suddenly break down under a flood of questions. He looked at her once again and admired her profile. From her chin, his eyes wandered to a beautiful brooch she had pinned over her right breast...a wide, glistening border, artfully filled with a finely worked filigree of silver. He rubbed his chin again, annoyed at the stubble.

"We had planned to get more information about AIDS from a doctor. But we don't need to do that, now. You have informed us completely." He looked at her with genuine admiration. "I must say, you seem to have a good deal of information."

She gestured nonchalantly.

"Not too hard to understand. I had a brother who suffered from the disease. Besides I'm confronted with AIDS on a regular basis in my work."

"What is it you do?"

"I'm a registered nurse at St. Matthew's Hospital."

DeKok narrowed his eyes.

"You work with Dr. Hardinxveld?"

An alert look came in her eyes.

"Do you know him?"

DeKok shook his head.

"No, I don't know him, I've only heard his name mentioned."

9

The next morning DeKok entered the detective room in a cheerful mood and with a closely shaven face. A good night's rest had revived his spirits and banished the tired lethargy to the deep recesses of his memory. At first he had trouble falling asleep. One hundred thousand in valid currency around a boy's waist...a death of AIDS on a sofa...a cruelly murdered man in a doorway...a Taurus instead of a Capricorn...a strangely shaped wound...shards of conversation...stupid threats. It all revolved around in his head like a runaway carousel.

At first he tried to sharpen the images and memories, to discover a connection, any connection. How were Hardinxveld, Marianne Hoogwoud, her father, and Abbenes related? Did their paths cross at St. Matthew's Hospital, Amstel Land or both? Were the connections coincidental? Or was Amsterdam, despite its importance, really a small town? The population was somewhere between a half million and a million people, depending on the number of tourists in a given season. It was inevitable some would touch each other's lives. He knew all this would resolve itself somehow, it always did. It's a small world, after all, he concluded with a smile.

Finally, after about half an hour, he gave it up and dozed away. His wife's melodic, refined snore made a comforting sound in the background. In the morning he awoke refreshed.

He threw his old hat in the direction of the peg on the wall and missed by about three feet. Laughing at his failure he picked it up and hung it properly on the hook. Then he turned toward Vledder. The young man was seated behind his computer, typing rapidly, as one possessed. When he noticed DeKok, he rested his fingers, grabbed a piece of paper from a stack of notes, and stood up.

"I have Martha's address," he announced.

"How did you get that so quickly?"

"The police in Utrecht."

"When did you call them?"

Vledder shook his head.

"I never got the chance, they called here."

"How did they know we were interested?" DeKok asked, surprised.

"They didn't know," admitted Vledder. "Last night a young woman, a Martha Maria Hooglied, contacted the police." He grabbed another scrap of paper from his desk. "She said that her belief in the Lord did not allow her to remain silent on certain subjects. She wanted to clear her conscience and said she was prepared to speak out on the murder of a lawyer in Amsterdam, a Mr. Abbenes."

"And?"

"What?"

"Did they take her statement?"

"No."

"Why not?"

Vledder looked perplexed.

"They tried several times, but she only wants to talk to you, Inspector DeKok of Warmoes Street Station."

DeKok's eyebrows suddenly came alive. Vledder watched, fascinated, as his partner's eyebrows suddenly danced across his forehead like two drunken, fuzzy caterpillars.

The display ended almost as soon as it started when DeKok began to speak.

"She asked for me? DeKok?"

Vledder nodded, while glancing at the scrap of paper in his hand.

"That's what she said. Somebody must have given her the name." Vledder sighed. "Our colleagues in Utrecht tried to reach us last night, but we had already gone home. And you must have been sleeping like a puppy dog. Nobody answered the phone at your house."

DeKok grinned.

"I didn't hear a thing."

"Well," continued Vledder, "from what I understand, Martha must have caused some problems for the guys in Utrecht. When they couldn't reach you, they didn't quite know what to do. They tried to find an excuse to hold her, but they could not legally charge her with anything. In the end they had to let her go. But they did get her address, and that's what they phoned through this morning. Luckily I was here."

"Where's the address?"

"Oh, right here," Vledder said, purposefully handing it over.

DeKok read the note.

"Cleopatra Drive," he said out loud. He thought for a minute and turned to get his coat and hat. "Let's go," he offered over his shoulder.

"Where to?" Vledder asked dimly.

"Utrecht, of course." He pushed his hat on his head. "Or don't you believe Martha has a conscience?"

DeKok looked at the woman in the door opening. Little Lowee was right, he thought. She looked like a prim, proper person. Dressed in black, with a high-closing blouse and a skirt that was just a little too long—she seemed stiff, unapproachable. A severe part in her hair caused the dark-blonde hair to hang on either side of her head. But her elfin face and large, brown eyes emanated peace and friendliness. The old inspector held his head to one side.

"Martha Maria Hooglied?"

She looked at him with just a hint of uncertainty.

"That is my name."

DeKok smiled a winning smile.

"My name is Inspector DeKok, with a kay-oh-kay." He pointed a thumb over his shoulder. "My colleague, Vledder. We're from Amsterdam. The police here in Utrecht called us. You indicated that you would be prepared to tell us about the murder of Mr. Abbenes, the lawyer."

She stepped aside and made a beckoning gesture.

"Please, come in."

DeKok hesitated for a moment.

"Are you alone?"

Her large, brown eyes looked a question.

"Who else would be here?"

"Franciscus Kraay."

She shook her head.

"Frankie and I are not married," she said, chiding him like a teacher correcting a student. "And I wonder if we ever will be."

DeKok looked surprised.

"Has the affair ended?"

Martha's friendly eyes suddenly spat fire.

"There has never been any question of an affair," she reacted sharply. "Frankie and I are friends within, eh, appropriate limits."

DeKok nodded.

"The bedroom is taboo."

"Precisely."

The grey sleuth passed her in entering the house. The sharp exchange had not pleased him. He always tried to start out politely, formally. In this case, however, he had judged it advisable to get some idea of the relationship between this prim lady and The Crow right away. Certainly the two were polar opposites. Frankie was a primitive man with a hasty, nasty, temper. DeKok believed Franciscus Kraay capable of murder. As he waited for Martha to close the door, he pushed out his lower lip. He wondered whether the murder of Abbenes was the deed of an impulsive, primitive individual?

Martha had closed the front door and now led the way to a cozy living room. Some rattan chairs with flowery cushions looked inviting. A number of small dressers stood against the walls, each covered with a wide variety of figurines in white ceramic.

"Hooglied," he started. "A beautiful name for a devout woman."

Martha nodded comfortably.

"King Solomon has said some beautiful things about women."

DeKok smiled, noting to himself "Hooglied" is Dutch for the *Song of Solomon*, high song.

"Solomon was a connoisseur." He gave her a questioning look. "Is Frankie a connoisseur?"

"What do you mean," she asked icily, "as a Bible student, or as a connoisseur of women?"

DeKok remained silent. He found it difficult to plan a strategy with this woman. To gain some time, he rubbed the back of his neck.

I...eh, I have known Franciscus Kraay for a long time. I knew him professionally years ago, a strong man with an uncontrollable urge to do things. If he needed to hit somebody, he did. His knowledge of the Lord was limited to a few phrases that can only be considered blasphemous."

A smile lit up her face.

"His knowledge of women," she said delicately, "is at the same level."

DeKok glanced at Vledder. He wished the young inspector would take over the interrogation. But Vledder leaned comfortably back in his chair, his notebook on one knee, pen poised above it. He did not notice DeKok's glance. DeKok rubbed his little finger against the bridge of his nose.

"How did you meet Frankie?"

"During an ear evening."

DeKok's eyes widened.

"An ear evening?" he repeated, puzzled.

Martha nodded.

"We meet twice a week for a so-called ear evening with a few church people." Her gestures became lively. "There are so many speakers in the world, but so few listeners. We prefer to be speaking ourselves. Therefore we're not usually prepared to lend an ear."

"Aha, thus, they are *ear* evenings."

She entwined her fingers and placed her hands in her lap.

"The evenings are usually well attended. There are so many people around us in need, more than you might suspect." She paused and changed her tone of voice. "One evening I was the ear for Franciscus Kraay."

"He was in need?" asked DeKok.

She nodded almost imperceptibly.

"You could say that. He told me his wife had been unfaithful to him. He said the lawyer who handled the divorce had betrayed him." Her face was serious as she looked at DeKok. "In my whole life," she continued softly, "I have never met a man who carried as much hate as did Frankie."

"He hated Abbenes?"

She covered her eyes with her hands.

"It was consuming. Frankie felt betrayed, swindled, and debased by the lawyer. Women, he said, can be expected to be unfaithful. That was, as Frankie said, part of their nature. But an attorney is an officer of the court and is supposed to serve justice. 'One doesn't mess around with justice,' he said."

DeKok grinned broadly.

"A widely held misunderstanding." It sounded unbelievably cynical. He leaned forward. "Did Frankie make any threats?"

Martha sighed deeply.

"That night I prayed fervently that Frankie would not meet that lawyer again, at least not for years."

"You were afraid of consequences?"

"Certainly. Frankie is a powder keg. He was in such a state of spiritual confusion. His intense hatred for that man could have burst forth at any moment."

"You could have referred him to a psychiatrist."

"I did. But Frankie wouldn't hear of it. When I insisted, he became angry. He asked me if I thought he was crazy. He wasn't a 'head case,' as he called it."

DeKok looked sympathetic.

"That willing, listening got you into a lot of trouble."

She gave a tired smile.

"That is the risk of which I was aware the moment I decided to participate in the ear evenings at the church."

DeKok lifted a hand, but then let it drop.

"But in the end, you took him into your heart...you cared."

Martha hesitated.

"Yes," she admitted after a long pause. "You could say that. I was worried and filled with pity. For such a big, strong man, he was so vulnerable. I made an appointment with him for the next day. We traveled to Amsterdam together because he wanted to. I saw the neighborhood were he grew up and that explained a lot. He grew up between Sodom and Gomorrah."

DeKok swallowed. He had a sharp retort on his tongue, but controlled himself.

"I take it," he said carefully, looking for the words, "you tried repeatedly to change Frankie's mind, to encourage nobler thoughts?"

She blushed.

"Of course I tried, several times." She raised her voice, becoming more emotional. "I tried and I tried. It isn't okay to just stand back and let somebody become a murderer."

The last remark touched DeKok. He remained still while he looked at her closely. He noticed every expression, every movement.

"Mr. Abbenes is dead," he said hard, with compelling tone in his voice. "Murdered."

Martha Hooglied lowered her head.

"I know," she said, sobbing. "I know. He was killed with a golf club."

10

Slightly confused for a moment, DeKok looked from Martha to Vledder and back again.

"A golf club?" He was unable to keep the tension out of his voice. "You said a golf club?"

Martha Hooglied looked up with a teary face and nodded.

"That's what he was going to use."

"Frankie The Crow?"

She nodded again.

"He told me exactly what he intended to do." Her eyes again filled with tears. "And now he has done it, too."

DeKok gave her a searching look.

"Are you certain?"

With the back of her hand she wiped the tears out of her eyes.

"I read it in the paper, yesterday. Mr. Abbenes, renowned attorney, found murdered on the doorstep of his office."

"Then you knew Frankie had completed the next installment of his threat," said Vledder.

Martha looked at him as if she just noticed his presence. Then looked away and walked to one of the dressers and took a handkerchief from a drawer. She worked on her face.

"It should never have gone that far," she said softly, still facing the wall. She turned around. "It's all my fault," she said as she returned to her seat.

"I should have been able to convince him that revenge is a sin against God," she went on, after she was seated. "God will punish the unjust Himself. As it reads in the Bible, 'Vengeance is mine, sayeth the Lord.'"

DeKok pursed his lips. He looked at Vledder, who shrugged. The shrug indicated that the he did not know what else to say and at the same time apologized for the interruption. DeKok returned his attention to the woman.

"Perhaps Frankie did not want to wait?" he said.

She looked puzzled.

"Did not want to wait for what?"

"The vengeance of the Lord."

She wiped the handkerchief over her face. Her mouth became a thin line.

"You shouldn't mock belief in God," she said waspishly.

DeKok shook his head.

"I don't," he corrected calmly. "But it is fact that impatient people sometimes find Heavenly intervention a bit, ahem, a bit long term."

Martha showed some spirit. Her eyes sparked again.

"When seen in the light of eternity—"

DeKok waved her words away. He regretted his remarks. He hadn't intended to spark a religious discussion. That was not why he had come to Utrecht. He spread both hands.

"What was Frankie's plan?"

She thought, momentarily stunned by the abrupt change of direction.

"He planned," she said warily, "to trick Abbenes to meet him at his office, after hours. Then he planned to wait for him and knock him out with a golf club."

"Why choose a golf club?"

A sad smile played around her lips.

"Frankie thought the golf club was a brilliant idea. He was actually proud of it."

"Proud...why?"

She stuffed the handkerchief in a sleeve of her blouse and sat up straight.

"Frankie knew," she continued, "that Mr. Abbenes was a dedicated golfer." She took a deep breath. "As far as Frankie was concerned, golf was a game for the rich. Only they had the time and the money for it...the money for all the equipment."

"Such as golf clubs?"

She nodded, almost absent-mindedly.

"Ordinary people don't posses that sort of equipment. Therefore, if the police were to discover that Abbenes had been killed with a golf club, they would never think of Frankie."

DeKok narrowed his eyes. Knowing Frankie it was a cunning plan. He pensively bit his lower lip.

"How did Frankie get the murder weapon?"

"He bought it in a sports store," she answered, shrugging.

"Did he ever show it to you?"

She shook her head.

"No, he had that thing at home. I've never been there, on principle."

DeKok leaned forward. His attitude was confidential.

"If I understood you correctly," he said slowly, pensively, "you went to the police last night, after you had read in the newspaper that Mr. Abbenes had been murdered."

Her glance drifted away.

"I didn't go immediately. I had to struggle with myself—wasn't sure what I should do."

DeKok feigned amazement.

"You contemplated letting a murderer stay on the street?"

She nodded slowly.

"I thought hard about the consequences of that ear evening. Frankie obviously needed to discuss his murderous plans with somebody. In fact, that night I functioned as his confessor."

DeKok raked his hand through his hair.

"And you thought of the sanctity of the confessional?"

"Yes, that was on my mind. The information was given to me in confidence."

DeKok did not react at once. He leaned back in his chair. With a meditative look he stared at the serene face in front of him and again he had the feeling he was approaching it the wrong way. He was missing something.

"When Frankie told you his plans," he asked finally, "did you warn Mr. Abbenes?"

Her eyes were suddenly frightened.

"I did not."

DeKok stood up. From his height he looked down at her.

"Why not?" he asked in a friendly, soothing tone of voice. "You knew he was in danger. Perhaps you could have prevented a murder."

Martha seemed to shrink, her body shook.

"I never thought," she sobbed, "Frankie would really do it."

As usual, Vledder was behind the wheel of the police VW as they left Cleopatra Street in Utrecht. He scowled as he followed the road signs leading to the main artery between Utrecht and Amsterdam. Utrecht is in the center of The Netherlands. In addition to numerous secondary roads, seven interstate highways converge on the old university town. The center of the town, however, retains its narrow streets as it has for more than five hundred years. To get out of Utrecht is to get out of a maze.

As they reached the highway, it started to rain. Vledder turned on the windshield wipers and DeKok sank down in the seat. The wipers always had a hypnotic effect on him. He dozed off.

Vledder glanced aside at his partner. Apparently he did not have a worry in the world. He seemed fast asleep. While he drove, Vledder mulled over the interview with Martha Hooglied. It had made a deep impression on him. The Crow, it was understood, had left his business in Utrecht and was not to be found. He had broken off all contact with Martha—made himself scarce. Was Frankie's flight an indication of guilt?

Amsterdam was already in sight when DeKok pressed himself more upright in the seat.

"Do you think it's possible?" he asked.

Vledder's thoughts were rudely interrupted.

"What?" he asked, keeping his eyes on the road.

"A golf club?"

Vledder had learned how to react to DeKok's seemingly random remarks.

"I think so," he said slowly. "I don't play golf, but I know there are different shaped clubs. The variety in putters, alone, is mind boggling. But the wound did have a characteristic shape. It could very well have been caused by a golf club. There are ways to prove it."

DeKok thought about that for awhile.

"Do we have the pictures that were taken in the morgue?"

"Yes, you pushed the envelope into a drawer before looking at them."

"Did you look at them?"

"I just glanced."

"Perhaps we can have them enlarged to actual size and then compare the wound to the end of a golf club."

"What kind of club?"

"What do you mean?"

"There are woods," lectured Vledder, "which are used for long distances, and irons, which, depending on the shape, can be used for specific distances. Then there are special clubs, for getting out of sand traps or—"

"And where did you acquire all this knowledge?" DeKok interrupted, slightly annoyed.

"I did some research."

"All right, can we get a sample of all the possible clubs to compare with the picture?"

"Maybe. I don't know where we would get them all. Besides, do you really think we could compare all these clubs to the picture of the wound?"

"Yes, well, in the old days we used to prepare and preserve the head as an exhibit for the court. But it created a lot of problems with the surviving families."

Vledder smirked.

"We would have to bury Abbenes without a head."

They fell silent as Vledder concentrated on the traffic in the suburbs. The rain increased and Vledder increased the speed of the wipers.

It was DeKok's turn to mentally review the meeting with Martha. Despite all he knew, he fervently hoped Frankie had not committed the murder of Abbenes. It would, he reflected, have consequences for the young woman. On the surface it seemed she had acted out of concern for Frankie. But she had also remained passive. And the law was unrelenting in that respect. Article 136 of the Criminal Code made it clear that Martha, having knowledge of a planned murder, should have warned the prospective victim and/or police. Now that the murder had actually been committed, she could be charged with a crime of omission. In other words she was an "accomplice *outside* the fact." It carried the same penalty as an "accomplice *after* the fact." DeKok sighed.

"With Martha's statements, should the murder weapon indeed turn out to be a golf club, Frankie is in deep trouble."

Concern was in his voice and Vledder reacted with biting sarcasm.

"You're actually worried about him, aren't you?"

"What?"

The young inspector slapped the steering wheel with one hand.

"Martha's line of drivel worries you."

DeKok looked genuinely surprised.

"What drivel?"

Vledder shook his head angrily.

"I feel no pity whatsoever."

"For whom?"

"Kraay, of course. As far as I'm concerned he's no more than a predacious killer. He's driven by hate and revenge.

He calmly plans a cunning murder. The sentimental slobber offends me. If anyone had consulted me, we'd have gone straight to the Utrecht police. We'd have sent out an APB for him on the spot, requesting location, apprehension, and transportation to Amsterdam." He glanced aside, his face red with anger.

DeKok resignedly let Vledder's words pass him by.

"You and Frankie have no past," he defended weakly. "But *I* know him. I had a lot of contact with him in the old days. That's why...that's why I find it difficult to see him as a killer."

Vledder remained testy.

"I *don't* know him," he said with emphasis. "But your memory of Frankie back in the day is not a measure of the man. That's an illusion. He may have been politically naïve and high on the Ape Index, but that was long ago." Vledder took a deep breath. "Just think about it. He had the guts to leave the neighborhood where he grew up and where he was accepted. He had the savvy to build a successful business in strange surroundings. You, all of you, underestimate the man. He's exceptionally capable."

"You really think him capable of murder?"

Vledder nodded with an angry face.

"Yes!"

11

Commissaris Buitendam rose hastily from his chair. He offered a welcoming smile and an outstretched hand to DeKok.

"I asked you to stop by, DeKok," he said in his usual aristocratic voice, "because I felt called upon to congratulate you for your success."

DeKok looked surprised and ignored the outstretched hand.

"What success?"

The commissaris changed his gesture to a jovial wave.

"You've solved the murder of Mr. Abbenes. I saw the APB that asked for a man's location, apprehension, and transportation to Amsterdam as a murder suspect. Of course, I immediately informed our judge advocate. Mr. Schaap was overjoyed." He sat down. "Personally I always felt the perpetrator was to be found among the widespread clientele of Mr. Abbenes. And that turned out to be true. I understand from Vledder this Franciscus Kraay was unhappy about the behavior of the attorney. Thus he came to do his evil deed out of personal revenge."

DeKok narrowed his eyes.

"You've already talked to Vledder?"

The chief nodded.

"I encountered him in the corridor. I complimented

him as well for this success. I must say, a remarkable achievement!"

DeKok feigned confusion.

"You are referring to the murder?"

Laughing, Buitendam shook his head.

"I mean finding the perpetrator."

"We don't have him yet."

"A matter of time, I am certain. In our densely populated country he'll surface, if not today, tomorrow."

DeKok nodded slowly to himself.

"I hope tomorrow."

The commissaris looked at him with suspicion. He had noted DeKok's tone of voice and was not pleased with what he heard.

"Why tomorrow?"

DeKok grinned.

"That will give me a whole day to find the real murderer."

Buitendam paled.

"That, eh, that Franciscus Kraay is *not* the murderer?"

DeKok rubbed his chin.

"I'm sorry," he said somberly, "but I don't feel he's the killer. Frankie is not our man."

The commissaris grinned without mirth.

"What about the APB?"

The gray sleuth waved that away.

"From a strictly judicial point of view it was perfectly legitimate." He leaned his head to one side. "Sometimes an old inspector must humor an overly enthusiastic, younger colleague. It is especially important when the junior officer wishes to make an overeager commissaris happy."

Buitendam stood up. Red spots appeared high on his

cheeks. His nostrils trembled. With a wild gesture he pointed at the door.

"Out!" he screamed.

When DeKok returned to the detective room, he lowered himself behind his desk with a sigh. Vledder looked at him.

"You went too far again, eh?"

"Whatever can you mean?"

"The commissaris sent you from the room again, right?"

DeKok nodded with a sad face.

"He does it every time," he admitted timidly. "The man should have more self-control."

Vledder rolled his eyes.

"And he wanted to congratulate you with solving Abbenes' murder."

DeKok shook his head.

"That's a misunderstanding. The murder isn't solved at all."

Vledder's face fell.

"Are you starting up again?" he exclaimed, irritation in his voice. "I thought we had discussed this at length in the car?" With a gesture of resignation he raised both hands in the air. "After all, you agreed to send that APB?"

"Of course," agreed DeKok. "We have to talk to Frankie. We have to ask him some questions. For instance, I'd like to know why he didn't bash in Sophie's skull?"

"You're talking about his ex-wife?"

"Exactly. If Frankie is not the primitive, impulsive wild man Martha, Lowee, and I know, then he's a cunning, deliberate killer. If he truly is capable of anything, why did he murder his attorney instead of his wife?"

"That's obvious. Revenge."

DeKok grinned broadly.

"What is the financial return for revenge? Zero! A truly cunning Frankie would have killed his demanding ex-wife. One blow and he would have been rid of his heavy alimony payments. He could have quietly continued his successful business."

Vledder's eyes widened.

"We have to warn her."

"Who?"

"Sophie, his ex."

"Why?"

"She's his next victim. She's almost certainly the next installment."

"Installment?"

"Sure he threatened *installments*, don't you remember? First came the threat, then a killing, next another killing. If his wife is next, who will follow her?"

DeKok stood up and walked away. He grabbed his coat and hat in passing. Vledder followed him.

"Where are you going now?"

DeKok did not answer the question directly. He gestured at his desk.

"Bring along those photos of the head wound and ask if Weelen will meet us at Amstel Land, the golf club."

"Amstel Land?"

DeKok placed his hat on his head and nodded.

"I want to see with my own eyes the sort of things one uses to hit a little ball."

DeKok's admiring glance roamed around the central lobby of the clubhouse. The space was comfortably furnished and decorated. To one side was a magnificent teakwood bar. Comfortable chairs were grouped around low tables, providing inviting conversation nooks. The walls were decorated with original paintings by René Broné, the American sports painter.

Large, floor-to-ceiling windows gave a panoramic view of the undulating golf course, where a landscape artist had planted trees and bushes. The trees waved gently in the breeze against a cloudless blue sky.

Mr. Oude, the secretary of Amstel Land, a gregarious man with a slight Frisian accent, received the inspectors in his large office. He revealed himself as an entertaining conversationalist, telling them about the day-to-day operations of the club with a touch of humor. After that, he accompanied them courteously to the bar area, awaiting the arrival of Father Hoogwoud, the greenskeeper. Vledder worried nervously with his necktie.

"I'm not interested in old Hoogwoud. I want to see the rest of the club."

"That will come later," soothed DeKok. "We'll ask Mr. Hoogwoud to take us to the resident pro. We're waiting for Bram Weelen, anyhow."

"Well I can understand Frankie on at least one point. He says golf is a sport for the idle rich. It must cost a fortune to maintain so much open space in our densely populated country."

"Yes, the dues must be astronomical. Good farm land, this is," nodded DeKok. "But I believe, in other countries, notably England and the United States, golf is a more, eh, egalitarian sport. They even have municipal golf courses."

"Even so it all seems a waste of time and money to me."

"That's because you're not one of the idle rich," mocked DeKok.

"Yes," growled Vledder, "and never likely to become one."

DeKok rose to his feet. An older man limped past the imposing fireplace and approached their table. The man progressed slowly. His left leg had trouble catching up. When he came nearer, a smile of recognition played around his lips.

"The description was accurate. You're Inspector DeKok from Warmoes Street. I've heard a lot about you. It's a pity you had to be involved with my family under these unpleasant circumstances."

The gray sleuth shook the proffered hand. Then he waved at one of the chairs around the table.

"Please sit down. Since I'm here anyway, I asked the secretary for an introduction. I've wanted to meet you for some time."

With stiff movements and a pain-distorted face, Hoogwoud sank down in the easy chair.

"I want to apologize," he said with a sigh, "for the behavior of my son, Casper. I understand he has been rather discourteous to you, arrogant and uncooperative." He smiled sadly. "A father always hopes his children become pillars of the community...honorable and respected."

DeKok studied the man. Hoogwoud, he thought, did not look healthy; he was thin and gray, with sunken cheeks. Only his clear, blue eyes showed alert under his bushy eyebrows.

"You feel you have not succeeded as a father?"

Old Hoogwoud shrugged his shoulders.

"You can lead children up the righteous path, but that's about all. There's no guarantee they'll follow it." He stared into the distance for a moment and then smiled tenderly. "Marianne has grown up to be a caring young woman. She gives me a lot of support. With the boys I was less lucky." His face fell. "Marcel wanted to leave the house at a very early age, and Casper, well, you've met him—a self-satisfied brat."

"He blames your despotic ways," DeKok said evenly.

Hoogwoud shook his head in a melancholic way.

"It's an empty slogan. He's parroting the catchphrase of modern youth." It sounded bitter. "They lose sight of reality and turn things around. I would never have become *despotic*, as he calls it, if the boys had respected me as their father. 'Honour thy father and thy mother; that thy days maybe long upon the land which the Lord thy God giveth thee.' It is the Fifth Commandment. But the boys never obeyed it. They did not honor their father." Tears came into his eyes. "And Marcel's days were short."

"God's hand?"

Hoogwoud produced a handkerchief and dabbed his eyes.

"The ways of the Lord are mysterious," he said evasively.

DeKok rubbed his face with a flat hand. He realized that for the second time during this investigation he was about to get entangled in a religious discussion. It was time to change the subject.

"Let me ask about Mr. Abbenes. Did you know him well?"

Hoogwoud nodded with conviction.

"He came here often, almost every day, to meet his friends."

The gray sleuth raised his hand with spread fingers and counted off as he spoke: "Dr. Hardinxveld, Mr. Darthouse—" he stopped.

" —and Mr. Leem," supplied Hoogwoud.

"Leem...Leem? I haven't heard that name before."

Hoogwoud's gray face was lit up by a smile.

"Mr. Leem is the minister of a large church, here in town. He's been a member for many years. I knew his father. Mr. Leem is also a member of the Four-Leaf Clover, the Clover Quartet. Or, as we sometimes mockingly say, the Sex Quartet."

DeKok relaxed.

"Sex Quartet," he laughed. "Did the gentlemen mix sex with their golf?"

Hoogwoud gestured vaguely.

"Ach, you know how these things happen among members of a club. There's alot of gossip; it is to be expected. People whispered about the gentlemen organizing parties among themselves."

"Aha, and the parties include ladies."

A naughty twinkle appeared in Hoogwoud's eyes.

"I presume so. But with one important exception—their *own* ladies."

DeKok nodded resignedly.

"The mothers of the children stay at home."

Hoogwoud spread his hands. His face became serious.

"You should not leap to a false conclusion because of what I say. I mean, I don't know whether the parties are fact or fiction." His eyes twinkled again. "I have certainly never been invited."

DeKok waved around at the surroundings.

"They wouldn't have held the parties here?"

Father Hoogwoud shook his had.

"Absolutely not," he said, sounding offended. "The trustees would never have permitted it. Impossible."

DeKok rubbed his nose with his little finger.

"What else kept the gentlemen together? Naming the relationship after a four-leaf clover seems to indicate a tight relationship."

"They were all close friends. For years they came here to the course to hit balls. I'm convinced they then passed the balls from one to the other in business and social circles."

DeKok smiled at the play on words. He looked again at old Hoogwoud's face and found empathy there. He measured the light in his clear, blue eyes. DeKok suspected the old man's frail body housed more spiritual power than one would suspect at first glance. Casper's verdict rang in his mind: *An old-fashioned patriarch with outdated ideas about raising a family.* Was that right?"

DeKok stood up and extended a helping hand to the old greenskeeper.

"Shall we visit the pro?" He glanced aside. "I think my young colleague is getting annoyed with our casual chat."

They left the bar, gearing themselves to Hoogwoud's speed. A short distance from the main clubhouse they found a good-sized shop, packed to the rafters with golf equipment. Hoogwoud introduced the inspectors to a tall, slender young man in his early twenties.

"This is Rudy, one of our young professionals. What he doesn't know about golf, is not worth knowing."

The young man laughed.

"*Dad* Hoogwoud exaggerates."

DeKok produced an envelope from a large inside pocket of his raincoat and placed it in front of the young man.

"Inside there are pictures," he explained, "of Mr. Abbenes' wound, caused by an object hitting the skull. The blow was immediately fatal, and we presume that it was made with a golf club."

The young man studied the photos carefully, visibly horrified. His index finger traced the contours of the wound.

"That mark," he said pensively, but with assurance, "could be a five iron, or maybe a nine or seven iron."

"Did you say a seven iron?" repeated Hoogwoud, shocked.

The young man nodded calmly.

"Yes, but maybe one of the others, too. It's a little hard to be too specific with that kind of gash."

"Dr. Hardinxveld," Hoogwoud said softly.

"What about Dr. Hardinxveld?" DeKok asked with surprise.

The old man looked away from the photographs and looked at Vledder and DeKok.

"A seven iron is the club, he said, that disappeared from his bag."

12

Vledder steered the battered VW from between an aged Rolls Royce and a low, sleek Porsche.

DeKok sprawled in the seat next to him. He had listened attentively to the young golf pro. Vledder had only skimmed the surface with his golf research. A golf club, he now understood, was not just a golf club. DeKok shook his head in wonderment.

"Unbelievable that a stick with a lump of wood or metal at one end can have so many names," he said. It sounded somewhat disdainful.

Vledder glanced at him.

"If Bram Weelen does his job right," he said, "the evidence against Frankie is just about complete."

DeKok did not answer at once. He was a bit irritated by the stubbornness of his younger colleague.

"Don't you find it strange," he asked, after awhile, "that just a seven iron disappeared from Dr. Hardinxveld's golf bag?"

Vledder shrugged as if he did not care.

"I understand," he said nonchalantly, "that a seven iron is frequently used. Another member probably borrowed it."

DeKok grinned.

"Borrowed it to hit a ball, or to hit Abbenes' skull?"

Vledder was getting visibly agitated. His face turned red

and he gripped the steering wheel so tight that his knuckles stood out white against his skin.

"What would be the motive?" he asked pugnaciously. "Did Dr. Hardinxveld have a reason to kill Abbenes, or anybody else in the club? No," he answered himself. "But Franciscus Kraay *had* a motive *and* a plan. He also had the weapon—he bought a seven iron."

DeKok remained silent. He felt any further discussion would be fruitless. He did not ask, for instance, how Vledder knew the golf club Frankie bought was a seven iron. Instead he stared at the heavy traffic. It was already getting dark. He glanced at the clock on the dashboard. The trip to Amstel Land had taken longer than expected. Yet he was not dissatisfied.

He looked at Vledder. His face was still hard and stubborn, full of tension. The gray sleuth gave him a friendly smile.

"Tomorrow, first thing," he said calmly, "we're going to the sports store where Frankie bought his golf club. It does seem the better course of action. Then we will be less dependent on Martha's statement."

Vledder gave him a suspicious glance.

"You mean that?" he asked dubiously.

DeKok nodded, a grin around his lips.

"After all, we're working together on this murder, aren't we?"

As Vledder and DeKok entered the lobby of the station house, Jan Kuster looked up and beckoned them to the counter that separated the public area from the rest of the police station.

"Little Lowee has been here."

DeKok was surprised.

"He was?"

Kuster grimaced.

"Scrawny fellow, mousey face?" he asked with a grimace.

DeKok laughed.

"Yes, yes, of course, you know him as well. What did he want?"

"He wanted to speak with you. It was rather urgent, he said."

DeKok nodded to himself.

"Did he say anything else?"

The watch commander shook his head.

"He was a bit skittish. He blurted out his message and scurried away in seconds."

DeKok grinned.

"No doubt. Lowee has a severe allergy. He's allergic to police uniforms." He put a hand on Kuster's shoulder. "We'll go see him shortly. But first, we are going to get something to eat." He turned to Vledder. "Would you be willing to fix another plate of ham and eggs?"

"Sure," said Vledder. "I also do a mean omelette."

"No, the ham and eggs were perfect."

Vledder walked to the kitchen and DeKok climbed the stairs. It was extraordinary for Lowee to come to the station in person. He didn't like to be seen around the station. There was always the danger the underworld would label him as an informer.

DeKok idly wondered what urgent business the small barkeep had to discuss. It was hard to predict Little Lowee. He had connections all over Amsterdam, better connections than the police, thought DeKok with a wry smile.

He walked toward the detective room on the second floor. Slowly he divested himself of hat and coat and sat down behind his desk. A pink envelope was placed in the center of his desk. A feminine hand had written *Inspector DeKok*. There was no further address.

DeKok lifted the envelope to his nose and sniffed. There was the faint smell of a remembered perfume. He opened the envelope with a pencil and took a thick, pink sheet from the cover.

"Dear Inspector DeKok," he read out loud. "It is difficult to reach you by phone, so I am having this delivered. I request you return the pendant you found on my husband to me. I want to have it as a keepsake, to remember him by. Mrs. Abbenes. P. S. It is not a bull, but a calf."

The partners ambled companionably from Warmoes Street to Rear Fort Canal. The pace was picking up in the Red Light District. The sex entertainment business was nearly running at capacity. It was a mighty engine, generating millions of dollars a day. DeKok nudged Vledder with an elbow.

"It's not a little bull, but a calf."

Vledder's look was one of consternation.

"What did you say?"

"The little bull is a calf."

"What little bull?"

"The pendant Abbenes wore around his neck."

"Why did you bring *that* up?"

"That's what Mrs. Abbenes wrote. She wants the pendant back as a memory of her husband. She ended her note with a P. S.: *It is not a bull, but a calf.*

DEKOK AND MURDER BY INSTALLMENT   109

Vledder shrugged.

"Well, I don't see the difference. A young bull is also a calf. Or am I wrong?"

DeKok shrugged in turn.

"I'm not sure," he said hesitantly. "I grew up in a family of fishermen. I just thought it was strange, you see. That postscript to the note was completely superfluous. I feel it is some kind of cryptic message, something she wants to tell us."

Vledder reacted irritated.

"We're not here to crack codes. If Mrs. Abbenes wants to let us know something, she'd better use clear language."

DeKok nodded slowly, pensively.

"And yet," he said, "I find her behavior rather peculiar. When I visited her that morning, to offer my regrets for her husband's passing, she acted more like the 'Merry Widow' than a woman sorrowing over her lost husband." He paused, as if to gather his thoughts. "And I *still* don't understand why she happened to remember the conversation between Abbenes and Hardinxveld, when they discussed Casper Hoogwoud and his alleged fraud."

Vledder laughed carelessly.

"Once The Crow has confessed," he said airily, "you can forget all that."

DeKok did not react. He did not feel like another argument with his colleague.

Once they reached the corner of Barn Alley they entered Little Lowee's establishment. When the small barkeep noticed DeKok, he came from behind the bar and hurried over. His face was serious.

"Da Crow," he whispered.

DeKok leaned closer.

"What about Frankie?"

Lowee looked around, made sure Vledder was out of earshot.

"He's widdus Mom, onna canal."

Franciscus Kraay took the inspector by the lapels of his coat with both hands. There was fear and despair in his dark eyes.

"I didn't do it, DeKok," he yelled. "I did *not* do it. Believe me. I didn't do it. When I read it in the papers it scared me half to death."

DeKok took the hands from his lapels and pushed Kraay back into his chair. Frankie, he thought, had visibly aged. It seemed as if his mighty torso had sunk down to his hips. The lines in his face were sharper and deeper. His black hair was gray at the temples. DeKok straightened his lapels and sat down opposite the distraught man.

"Frankie, you had trouble with Abbenes. We know you threatened him."

Kraay grinned crookedly.

"What trouble? The slime ball cheated me. That's all there was to it."

"And nobody cheats The Crow."

Franciscus Kraay shook his head, calmer now. He had regained his composure.

"The Crow of today," he said conversationally, "is not The Crow of yesterday. The out-of-control wild man is gone. I haven't had anything to prove for many years."

DeKok smiled primly.

"That's true," he said with a smirk. "Today's Crow is much more cunning. He planned a refined way to do away with Abbenes. He bought a golf club."

Kraay looked surprised.

"You know that?"

DeKok spread his arms.

"My dear boy," he said genially, "we wouldn't drag you away from your mother unless we had clear evidence, sufficient for an arrest." He paused deliberately, let the tension build. "For what…for what did you need a golf club?"

Kraay became excited all over again.

"To crush Abbenes' skull—is *that* what you want to hear?"

DeKok folded his hands.

"I want to hear the truth. That's it, no more."

"I didn't do it."

"That's a song," said DeKok, "I have heard before. You're repeating yourself."

Kraay covered his face with his hands.

"Inspector, it *is* the truth."

DeKok lifted his index finger and studied it for a few seconds, as though he had never seen it before.

"All right," he conceded, "it is the truth. We'll take it as given, for the moment. Let's start again. You felt Abbenes cheated you. You bought a golf club, but not for golf?"

Kraay seemed to surrender. With a sigh he lowered his head. Only after several seconds did he lift it again.

"DeKok, will you listen to me?"

The inspector spread his arms wide.

"That's why I'm sitting here."

Kraay nodded to himself.

"It's true," he began softly, "I walked around for days planning to break that guy's head." He smiled sadly. "It's useless to deny it. I've said it so often and in so many places, I could as easily have taken an ad in the papers. In my defense, I suddenly saw everything I'd fought and worked to build taken away. It was more than any man could choke down, especially since I was innocent of wrongdoing. Who needs a no-good, cheating wife?" he asked, shrugging his shoulders. "What would most men do? I looked for a lawyer, a good one. I told the guy I wanted a divorce. It's a normal reaction, isn't it? While you're confiding in the lawyer you're not thinking you could be instantly ruined! No, but that's exactly what happened. One day I was on solid ground—financially, at least. The next, I was flat broke, forced to sell my business and—"

DeKok raised his hand to stop the flow of words.

"Get back to the golf club," he said caustically.

Kraay rubbed his dry lips with the back of his hand.

"I knew," he said, despair in his voice, "Abbenes was a fanatic golfer. He told me so himself. If you wanted to talk to him in his office, he was never there. Then Dungen, that dried-out clerk, would call the Amstel Land clubhouse. He always hung out there."

DeKok nodded.

"His obsession with golf gave you the idea to use a golf club as a weapon?"

Kraay lowered his head again.

"I once saw a sports program…two men were trying to hit each other with golf clubs. I thought—"

DeKok interrupted again.

"So, one evening, rather late, you called him on the phone and said you had to see him urgently. You waited for him near his office and when he—"

Franciscus Kraay jumped up. His face was red and his eyes protruded from their sockets.

"No!" he screamed. "No!"

The phone on DeKok's desk started to ring. The interruption was so sudden and overwhelming that Kraay and DeKok froze, staring silently at the instrument.

Vledder picked up on his extension and listened. His face suddenly became ashen. After a short time, he replaced the receiver.

DeKok turned toward him.

"Who was that?"

"The commissaris."

"And?"

"That woman called again."

DeKok narrowed his eyes.

"What did she say this time?"

"She said 'Darthouse is dead, not because of your righteousness, but because of mine.'"

13

The message shocked DeKok deeply. It took awhile before he could think clearly. He realized, at once, he could not discuss the matter with Kraay present. In a soothing gesture he placed a hand on the man's shoulder.

"I'm sorry, Frankie, but I can't let you go yet. I still don't know enough." His face became serious. "But I give you my word we won't keep you a minute longer than necessary."

Kraay swallowed. Tears welled in his eyes.

"I didn't do it," he said hoarsely.

DeKok tightened his grip on the man's shoulder.

"Frankie, you made a mess of things; you made them worse as you went along. Now you're faced with the consequences."

Kraay nodded timidly.

"You know what my problem is, DeKok? I have a big mouth."

The gray sleuth removed his hand.

"Be strong, Frankie." He beckoned to Vledder. "Take him downstairs and book him. Then come back here."

With his head almost lowered to his chest, Kraay walked to the exit of the detective room. Vledder followed him closely.

DeKok watched the duo disappear. He looked at the clock.

It was almost two o'clock in the morning. He reflected on the time—it coincided with Abbenes' murder. He picked up a phone book. He was still searching when Vledder returned. The young man looked depressed.

"I had him booked on suspicion of murder," he said dully. "Although I doubt his guilt more and more."

DeKok looked surpiised.

"And you were so convinced."

Vledder sighed.

"I thought him to be the ideal suspect."

DeKok shook his head.

"Not me. I never believed in his guilt."

"But you arrested him...you interrogated him."

DeKok nodded sagely.

"I've grown careful over the years. Feelings and facts don't always mix. Besides, an arrest was the only way to convince you."

Vledder looked contrite.

"I'm often too eager, too impulsive. I realized that again when I climbed the stairs after booking Frankie."

DeKok grinned.

"To improve the world, start with yourself."

"Something your old mother used to say?"

"No, I don't remember where I picked that up. I think it was written on the wall of some squatters building, awhile back. The wall was covered with admonitions such as 'Tomorrow is the first day of the rest of your life' and 'Make love, not war.' It was when we found Colette, you remember?"

"Colette? I don't recall."

"Colette was the woman killed by an overdose. We found her child."

"Oh, yes. Now I remember. It was the first and only time you used your computer."

"I did?"

"Yes, you had the baby on your desk and moved the screen to shield it from the harsh light of the ceiling."

They reminisced silently for a moment.

DeKok broke the short silence.

"Is the commissaris coming here?"

Vledder made a vague gesture.

"I think so, but he didn't say in so many words. Buiten-dam seemed a bit upset...shocked. He just said the woman had called again and repeated what she had said before."

"Darthouse is dead," repeated DeKok, "not because of your righteousness, but because of mine."

"Yes."

"That was it?"

Vledder shook his head.

"The commissaris did not tell me anything else. I don't think he *knows* anything else."

DeKok rubbed his chin.

"But there is an important difference between now and last time," he said thoughtfully. "Last time we had a dead Abbenes on his own doorstep, after which we got the message."

Vledder frowned.

"You're right. Now it's the other way around. We will have to look for the corpse. If the information from that woman is correct, there's a dead Darthouse, somewhere."

"Yes," nodded DeKok, "but where?"

Vledder put the key in the ignition.

"Where do you want to go?"

"Amstelveen. Emperor Charles Way 1721."

The young detective started the car and drove off.

"Who lives there?"

"While alive, Mr. Darthouse. I could not find his name in the Amsterdam phone book. Thankfully his residence was listed under Ijsselstein Bank."

Vledder turned the car around the corner.

"Wouldn't it have been easier to call Amstelveen? It would have saved time."

DeKok stared into the darkness.

"I like to see peoples' eyes while speaking to them." He turned toward Vledder. "Anyway what would I say over the phone? Something like, 'We heard your husband was murdered. Can you tell us the whereabouts of the body?'"

"Well, you'll have the same trouble when we get there."

DeKok made a helpless gesture.

"I don't have the professional touch like a priest, or a minister. I have to rely on intuition."

Vledder nodded.

"What if it is a joke?" he asked suddenly.

"What?"

"The announcement of the murder."

DeKok shook his head and sank down in the seat.

"No, it's no joke," he said somberly. "It was no joke when Abbenes was killed and it's no joke now. The text is so specific and direct. At this point my questions have to do with the caller's motives, her values. What 'righteousness' is she talking about?"

"Her own justice," Vledder sharply answered. "That's exactly what she says...means. Apparently the woman is not satisfied with our brand of justice."

DeKok scratched the back of his neck.

"Who is?" he asked rhetorically.

For awhile they drove on in silence. There was not much traffic on the road. Just a few taxis crossed their path from time to time. They passed the Olympic stadium on the left, soon reaching the suburb of Amstelveen and the wide, imposing Emperor Charles Way.

A few houses before 1721, Vledder found a parking space. As he pulled the key from the ignition, he looked up.

"That phone call from the commissaris has put us in an awkward position."

"How so?"

Vledder opened the driver's door.

"We know a murder has been committed, we know the name of the victim, but we have no evidence. We can't prove a thing. How long before Darthouse's corpse will surface?"

"Do you mean that figuratively, or do you think he's actually been pushed into a canal?"

"She could also have buried him."

"Why do you think it's a she?"

"Well," said Vledder, as they walked up to the house, "it *was* a woman who called."

Mrs. Darthouse looked with incredulity at the two men on her doorstep. She rearranged her pink dressing gown.

"Police inspectors from Amsterdam—is this not a strange hour for a visit?"

DeKok gave her a friendly smile.

"I understand your dismay."

Mrs. Darthouse ignored the remark and invited them in.

"Please have a seat," she said pleasantly, motioning to a

couple of dark brown, leather chairs. "How may I help you gentlemen?"

DeKok placed his hat on the floor next to his chair.

"My colleague and I," he began, feeling his way, "are in charge of investigating the Abbenes' murder. Although we have been at it for several days, we're still groping in the dark. We understand your husband was a friend of the deceased. A conversation with him could give us further insight...might prove helpful."

Mrs. Darthouse leaned against oaken wainscoating beside the brick fireplace. Her light green eyes gave the inspector a long, questioning look.

"You want to speak with my husband?"

"Indeed."

Her eyes narrowed and she looked at DeKok with suspicion.

"But didn't you discuss the subject with my husband at the bank?"

"Your husband told you that?"

"Certainly."

DeKok rubbed his chin.

"That conversation," he offered carefully, "was a bit disappointing. We were left with the impression your husband was holding something, eh, was not completely forthcoming."

She made a nonchalant gesture with her arm and readjusted her dressing gown.

"He must have had his reasons."

DeKok nodded and grinned crookedly.

"And we would like to know those reasons."

Mrs. Darthouse appeared to think about her answer. She walked to an easy chair from her place next to the fireplace.

DeKok watched the long, supple movement of her body as she seated herself elegantly. In the barely closed, pink dressing gown her exciting contours showed her figure to an advantage. She was a handsome woman, DeKok thought to himself, with an almost animal magnetism and grace. No doubt she was several years younger than her husband.

She crossed her slender legs.

"I have the feeling," she said pensively, "you are also holding something back."

"In what respect?"

Mrs. Darthouse leaned forward. DeKok felt captivated by her stare.

"Inspector DeKok, where is my husband?"

The old sleuth made an apologetic gesture.

"We...eh, we," he stumbled over the words. "We had hoped to find him here."

The soft expression on her face hardened. She raised her chin.

"You know very well he isn't here."

DeKok slowly raised an arm in her direction.

"Mrs. Darthouse, you don't know where he is?"

The young woman lowered her head. She suddenly looked defeated.

"I don't know," she whispered. "Really, I don't know. I'm just afraid."

"Why?"

"I'm afraid something has happened to him."

DeKok studied her.

"Is there a reason for your fear?"

She looked up at him.

"About an hour ago, my husband received a phone call.

I was already in bed. He came into the bedroom and told me he had to leave for awhile."

"He did not say where he was going?"

She shook her head.

"No, he just told me not to wait up for him. He wasn't sure how long it would take."

DeKok rubbed his face with a flat hand. He felt the conversation had reached a critical point. Further evasion was useless.

"I'm afraid," he said softly, compassion in his voice, "it may be a long time until he is back."

"I—I don't understand."

DeKok closed his eyes briefly.

"We have good reason to believe your husband has been the victim of an assault." He sighed. "He may have been murdered."

Her eyes became large and afraid.

"Murder?" she gasped.

DeKok nodded in confirmation.

"Someone, someone unknown, called our commissaris on the phone to say your husband was dead. We take the information seriously, extremely seriously. We received a similar message after the death of Mr. Abbenes."

Mrs. Darthouse swallowed.

"You, you think there is a connection?"

"We cannot exclude the possibility."

She rose from her chair. She paced the floor with her head bowed, wringing her hands.

"A connection," she repeated with despair in her voice, "a connection, but what *kind* of connection?"

DeKok shrugged his shoulders.

"Perhaps they both were involved in something."

Suddenly she stopped. Her mouth fell open. She looked at DeKok with a frightened expression on her face.

"That boy!" she cried.

"What boy?"

"The one who defrauded my husband's bank."

DeKok gave her a puzzled look.

"You mean Casper Hoogwoud?"

Mrs. Darthouse nodded fervently.

"Hoogwoud, yes, Casper Hoogwoud. Yes, my husband was afraid he would try to defraud the bank again. It was why he contacted Abbenes."

DeKok nodded his understanding. He picked up his hat from the floor and stood up.

"Thank you. Of course, we'll keep you informed," he said feelingly. "As soon as we know something more, we'll contact you."

Both inspectors walked toward the door. Just before he was to step out into the hall, DeKok turned around.

"Mrs. Darthouse, do you play golf?"

14

DeKok gave a last, long look at the stately Darthouse mansion. Then, in his typical, shuffling gate, he sped after Vledder. The young inspector looked around. He laughed. DeKok at speed was a comical sight.

When his thundering footsteps faded into the night, it was again intensely quiet on Emperor Charles Way. There was just the distant sound of an airplane, high in the sky.

Vledder pointed over his shoulder.

"Can we just leave her like that?"

"What do you mean?"

"You never know what will happen. The poor woman just learned her husband may have been the victim of a murderous attack."

DeKok gave him an unreadable look.

"What do you want to do? Go back and hold her hand?"

"Not a bad idea," Vledder offered. "I don't know how you see her, but in my eyes Mrs. Darthouse is a very attractive woman."

DeKok nodded.

"She's attractive and young."

Vledder opened the door for his mentor. There was a smile on his face.

"So attractive and young it seems a shame she would be chained to an older man the rest of her life."

"Exactly."

"That's why you asked if she played golf."

DeKok entered the car.

"Sometimes, Dick, you show signs of understanding life…a little."

Vledder slammed the door.

"Jump in the canal," he said with conviction.

They drove away from Amstelveen.

Vledder looked at his watch.

"It's almost three thirty. You still want to go back to the station?"

DeKok nodded.

"Perhaps some information has come in."

"You want me to radio in?"

"No. There's a good reason I don't want to radio in. I've told you before. Once they determine we sometimes use it, they'll be calling us constantly."

"Yes, well, that's why we have the radio."

"Bah, in the old days we never had radios. We still managed to get our messages across." He paused. "Of course, we did have call boxes, but they were only used for calling in. They couldn't reach you on those."

"Yes, yes," laughed Vledder, "you patrolled on foot and, if you did need a car, you hired a taxi. I've heard it all before. Were you not the one who walked five miles to school, every day, barefoot in the snow, uphill, both ways?"

DeKok laughed heartily.

"It wasn't all that bad. The island where I grew up was no more than two miles in length and barely a quarter-mile wide."

"It's still pretty thick in here. What sort of information

do you expect the office to have? You think they know where to find the corpse?"

DeKok became serious.

"I think," he said slowly, "Darthouse's corpse is not hidden at all. You see, I don't think the killer wants to keep his acts a secret. On the contrary he *wants* the world to know. That's why the weird phone calls."

A large truck suddenly emerged from a side road. Vledder braked suddenly to yield the right of way.

"Don't you find it strange," he asked as he shifted up again, "how we keep hearing references to Casper Hoogwoud every time we round a curve in this investigation? Even Mrs. Darthouse mentioned him."

DeKok grinned.

"Don't forget Darthouse emphatically denied knowing Hoogwoud and he denied the fraud with equal vehemence."

Vledder shook his head.

"It's hard to believe. Do you think Casper's story about the origin of that money could possibly be true?"

"You mean that *somebody*, some benefactor suddenly deposited the money in his account?"

He nodded.

"I was convinced he lied about it."

DeKok slowly rubbed the bridge of his nose with his little finger.

"Whatever the truth of the matter, the money stinks. Nothing will change my mind about it." He spread both hands. "In balance I find it difficult to see the money as motive for murder, double murder. The motive is not financial gain. Whatever drives this murderer, the motive is deeper, hidden."

"Do you think our murderer is a man?"

DeKok held an index finger up in the air.

"I'm certainly considering it," he spoke. "However, I also believe a woman would be just as capable of swinging a golf club. It would be a mistake to exclude the possibility that a man did the job. With or without help, a woman does enter the picture with the intriguing messages."

Vledder remained silent. He needed his full attention for the road, which was broken up and barricaded for a construction project.

"But that could mean that there are at least two people involved," he said when the road had cleared again.

"Exactly. At least two people are doing the Lord's will."

Vledder grimaced.

"The Lord's will?" he asked. "What are you saying?"

DeKok pressed himself up in the seat.

"Think about the message scripts. They always imply the murders were committed for the sake of righteousness, or a sort of justice."

Vledder glanced quickly aside.

"Are you talking executions?"

DeKok sighed deeply.

"Something like that."

"Heard anything?"

Jan Kuster, the watch commander, shook his head.

"Headquarters will let us know as soon as they get a report. I told the boys in our precinct to patrol all the canals slowly. We'll get a boat from the water police in the morning."

"Why the canals?"

"Wasn't the other guy found in the canal?"

"Yes, on Emperors Canal, but not in the water."

"Ah, well, it won't hurt to be extra alert."

DeKok nodded his understanding. The confusion was understandable, although Kuster should have known better. In Amsterdam, the quays on either side of the canals are named after the canal.

"Did the commissaris ever show up?"

Kuster grimaced.

"He was very ticked off because you didn't wait for him. According to him, he had left clear instructions."

"Where is he now?"

The watch commander pointed at the ceiling.

"Upstairs, in his office—he's with the judge advocate."

"Schaap?"

Kuster nodded unhappily.

"That one came about half an hour ago."

DeKok was surprised.

"Whatever can that man want in the middle of the night?"

Kuster looked grave.

"They're both interrogating Frankie The Crow."

"What!?"

Kuster snorted.

"They seem to think Frankie knows where he stashed Darthouse."

DeKok's face became expressionless. He pressed his lips together. Usually the gray sleuth was the epitome of amiability, but, when his superiors mixed in *his* investigations, anger rushed through his veins. It was one of the things that could unleash the berserker rage, the seldom seen explosive side of the placid Dutch.

He turned away from the counter and stepped toward

the stairs in long strides. He took the stairs two treads at a time. Vledder urgently wanted to prevent his friend from getting into trouble. Halfway up the stairs he overtook the old man and grabbed his raincoat.

DeKok turned around. His broad face was a steel mask. Slowly he shook his head.

"Can't you climb the stairs by yourself? Do I have to order you a cane?"

Vledder looked at him and laughed, relieved.

"I, eh, thought you were angry, recklessly angry."

In silence they climbed the rest of the stairs. On the second floor, DeKok walked toward the door of Buiten-dam's office. Without knocking he entered. When he stepped into the room he was again completely in control of himself. Amused, he beheld the three men around the low coffee table in the corner.

Commissaris Buitendam stood up, annoyed.

"I did not hear you knock," he said severely.

DeKok grinned.

"Could be I didn't knock."

The judge advocate pushed back his chair slightly and pointed at Franciscus Kraay.

"We decided to get the investigation moving, DeKok. Everything will be far easier," he announced primly, "if this man would just tell us where we can find the earthly remains of Mr. Darthouse. We don't want to have to search the entire city."

DeKok's eyes widened, feigning amazement.

"And *this man* knows where the body is?"

Mr. Schaap nodded with conviction.

"Of course he knows. A murderer always remembers where he leaves his victim." It sounded smug.

DeKok walked over to Frankie Kraay and motioned for him to stand up.

"Do you know the Ijsselstein Bank?"

Kraay stood up.

"I know *of* Ijsselstein Bank," he said evasively. "I don't have an account there, if that's what you mean."

DeKok ignored that.

"You've never been inside the bank?"

"No."

"What does the name Darthouse mean to you?"

Frankie shook his head and shrugged his shoulders.

"At first I thought it referred to a house where they play darts," he smiled. "But I have since learned it is the name of a dead man." He pointed at the commissaris and the judge advocate. "Them two say some Darthouse was murdered."

"And is that right?"

"How should I know?"

"Don't you know Darthouse?"

"No, never heard of him."

"So you did not kill a man by that name?"

Kraay placed a hand on his chest.

"Me?"

"Yes, you."

Kraay laughed unhappily. He sounded deeply embarrassed.

"Why would I kill a man I never even met? That's just crazy."

"And you're not crazy?"

"What do *you* think?"

DeKok seemed to look for inspiration from the ceiling. Then his eyes returned to Frankie.

"Then why," he asked with astonishment in his voice, "are these gentlemen bothering you?"

It was too much for Buitendam. He swallowed hard and his face became a familiar, furious shade of red. Before Kraay could answer DeKok's question, Buitendam pointed at the door.

When DeKok returned to the detective room, Vledder looked at him, shaking his head.

"Thrown out again?"

DeKok nodded sadly.

"He just can't control himself," he said somberly.

Vledder laughed.

"You're turning things around, as usual. The commissaris has never chased me from his room. It's your own fault. You always incite him. What was it this time?"

DeKok sat down in the chair behind his desk.

"The judge advocate made some scathing remarks regarding the conduct of the investigation and finding the corpse. So I took over interrogating Frankie. The way in which I did that did not please Buitendam. So, he sent me away. I certainly did not intend to offend him."

Vledder pulled his chair closer to the DeKok's desk.

"The commissaris and the judge advocate both believe Frankie is guilty?"

"That was my impression."

"Both murders?"

"Yes."

"Is that possible?"

DeKok shrugged carelessly.

"It would be wonderful for Frankie if we could

determine Darthouse was murdered while we were arresting him at his mother's house. That would give him an unbreakable alibi for the second murder. It would also cast doubt on his participation in Abbenes' murder."

"Why so?"

DeKok sat up straighter and played with a pencil on his desk.

"You must agree there is a clear connection between these two murders. Abbenes and Darthouse knew each other, undoubtedly shared interests and business connections. Both murders happened at night. The killer enticed each victim to leave home because of a telephone call. In each case our commissaris received a cryptic message from an unknown female caller."

Vledder nodded his agreement.

"The same perpetrator had to commit both murders. If Frankie didn't commit the second murder, he did not commit the first."

"Precisely."

"On the other hand if he did..." .

"In that case Frankie remains, technically, our prime suspect in both crimes."

Vledder grinned.

"Do you think Martha is the mystery woman with her own idea of justice?"

DeKok nodded and suddenly snapped the pencil in two.

"I find it highly unlikely *that* is the case. But it is possible...and we inspectors must, therefore, consider it."

Vledder looked at the large clock on the wall.

"Shall we go home? It's almost four thirty."

With a soft groan, DeKok rose from his chair. At that

moment Jan Kuster stormed into the room.

"They found the corpse of a man," he yelled from the door.

"Where?"

"Behind Wester Church. Someone bashed his skull in."

15

At eleven o'clock the next morning, a remarkably fresh, cheerful DeKok entered the station house at Warmoes Street. He was going on the strength of a few hours of sleep, a restorative hot-to-cold shower, and a good breakfast. Several cups of coffee had cured the last of the lethargy. He waved jovially at Meindert Post, the watch commander. Meindert had also been born on DeKok's island of Urk. He was too busy to notice DeKok.

DeKok found Vledder behind his computer in the large, crowded detective room. The young inspector looked hung-over. He was green around the gills, with dark rings under his eyes. When he saw DeKok, he produced a wan smile.

"A few more nights and days like this and I'll be ready for the glue factory. Then you'll have to work alone."

DeKok looked worried.

"Why are you here so early? Go back to bed."

"I can't," he sighed. "I made an appointment with Dr. Rusteloos, but first I have to finish this paperwork."

DeKok said nothing about the paperwork. Vledder had built a number of templates into the memory of his computer and could spit out any kind of report at a moment's notice. Vledder undoubtedly had everything lined up, and would be able to supply the ever-hungry bureaucracy with up-to-date information on the case. DeKok wondered how he had managed before Vledder took on all the paperwork. Despite DeKok's sense of relief, sometimes (like now) he could not help feeling guilty.

"What time is your appointment?"

"I should leave here in about half an hour." He looked up at DeKok.

"Now for the bad news: Frankie has escaped."

DeKok sat down, completely overwhelmed by the news.

"What?"

"Yes," nodded Vledder. "It happened last night, shortly after we left for Wester Church."

"But how?"

The young man shut down his computer and pushed the keyboard away.

"Kuster told me. When the commissaris and the judge advocate finished interrogating Frankie, they called the watch commander and asked him to come fetch him. Apparently the gentlemen felt it was taking too long and they decided to return Frankie to his cell by themselves." Vledder smirked. "No gloating—when they reached the upstairs corridor, Frankie hit the judge advocate a glancing blow, pushed the commissaris out of the way, and bolted for the stairs. Before either of them had recovered from the shock, the bird had flown."

"And what was the result of the interrogation?"

"Nothing. I haven't seen anything in writing. Haven't heard anything about it, either."

DeKok shook his head with disapproval.

"They probably drove Frankie crazy with their questions and he saw no way out but to flee."

"So, what now?"

DeKok scratched the back of his neck while he thought. The flight of Frankie was a development he had not foreseen.

"Too bad the coroner last night couldn't tell us more about the time of Darthouse's death." He spread his arms in a helpless gesture. "Dr. Koning is right. He never likes to make specific statements at the scene of the crime. It was rather chilly last night; body temperature alone would not have been enough. Worse still, the autopsy probably came too late to establish anything with certainty."

Vledder looked somber.

"We're not getting any breaks."

DeKok snorted.

"What can you expect? That the perpetrator will present himself stuffed, trussed, and garnished? I'll have mine with the usual, motive and evidence."

Vledder shook his head.

"Not going to happen, but sometimes it..." That was as far as he got. DeKok smiled. He took another good look at Vledder's pale face and the rings under his eyes. He stretched a finger in Vledder's direction.

"After the autopsy, you go straight home and to bed. I'll hear the report from Dr. Rusteloos tomorrow sometime."

Vledder protested.

"What if something important surfaces?"

DeKok shook his head.

"Tomorrow," he said with emphasis and walked over to get his coat and hat. Vledder was ready to leave, as well.

"Where are you going?"

DeKok turned around. His face was hard.

"I've promised myself," he said grimly, "a little talk with Dr. Hardinxveld."

A distinguished, gray-haired lady in a plain black dress shuffled on flat shoes ahead of DeKok. Her steps led down a corridor. She opened the door of a room, held the brass knob in her hand, and bowed him in.

"Sir will be with you shortly," she announced as if speaking of royalty.

Then she closed the door behind him and disappeared.

DeKok looked around. The room breathed nineteenth century respectability. There were exquisite tapestries, dark landscapes in gilt frames, an impressive wall of books. Baroque cherubs looked down from the ceiling. In the space between the two tall windows were some yellowed silhouettes in oval frames.

After a few minutes, a tall, slender man entered the room. DeKok estimated him to be in his early fifties. He wore a gray flannel suit and a red necktie on a pale blue shirt. With outstretched hand he approached DeKok.

"Hardinxveld," he said amiably. "I'm sorry to have kept you waiting. I was still at breakfast." He smiled pleasantly. "I am a night person, late to bed and late to breakfast." With a grandiose gesture he pointed at a set of Biedermeier easy chairs. "Let's sit down." He seated himself and crossed his long legs.

"Inspector DeKok," he said, as if savoring the sound. "Your name is well known. I understand you have a reputation for solving the most complex crimes."

DeKok nodded, not fooled by either the breezy attitude or the flattery.

"Your reputation creates obligations."

"I realize that."

DeKok studied the man in front of him. It was the hard,

intrusive scrutiny of a police officer. Dr. Hardinxveld had
a high forehead, sharply delineated face. His narrow nose
ended in wide nostrils above a set of full lips.

"Last night," began DeKok, "we discovered a corpse
on a quiet spot in the city. It was the corpse of a man who,
a little while earlier, had introduced himself to me as the
managing director of the Ijsselstein Bank."

Dr. Hardinxveld made a startled gesture.

"Goodness, now it's *Darthouse?*"

It sounded laconic, almost comical.

DeKok continued his scrutiny of the man's face.

"Are you not surprised?"

The doctor crossed his arms in front of his chest.

"Ach, no…not entirely. After what happened to Abbenes,
the murder of Darthouse was more or less in the realm of
expectation."

"I don't understand that."

Dr. Hardinxveld gestured vaguely around.

"Look, my dear man," he said with a sigh, "I don't fully
understand it myself; however, it seems incontrovertible
that some maniac is trying to wipe out all the members
of the Amstel Land Golf Club…preposterous, not to say
most annoying."

DeKok narrowed his eyes. Hardinxveld's reactions and
speech patterns puzzled him. He had difficulty measuring
the man.

"But you, yourself, are a member of Amstel Land. Aren't
you afraid you may be a victim at some future time?"

Hardinxveld nodded agreeably.

"Oh, yes, to be sure. It's entirely possible I would have
joined my forefathers, had I been so unwise as to follow the
instructions of a certain strange telephone call."

"Tell me more about the call."

"It was a woman, a stranger with a sexy voice. She asked me to meet her on Wester Market, behind Wester Church."

DeKok swallowed hard, trying to get his head around the fact Darthouse's body was found there. He leaned closer.

"The caller expected you to simply go?" he asked, skepticism in his voice.

"Yes, the day before yesterday."

"Why didn't you go?"

A smile danced around the full lips of the doctor.

"I knew what had happened to Abbenes, of course. He, too, had received such a phone call."

DeKok's face was expressionless.

"How do you know that?"

Hardinxveld spread his arms.

"Abbenes told me so."

"When?"

"The very evening."

"He was with you?"

Dr. Hardinxveld nodded in agreement.

"As I told you, I am a night person. It's my habit to go to bed late most nights. My friends know my habits. That evening, or I should say the small hours of the morning, close to two o'clock, Abbenes rang my doorbell. He said there was something wrong with his car. He thought it was the fuel line. He asked if he could borrow my Mercedes to get to a late appointment."

"It proved an appointment with death."

Hardinxveld waved that away.

"I can assure you, my good man, Abbenes did not know

it at the time. On the contrary, he was looking forward to a romantic intermezzo."

"With the woman who called?"

"Undoubtedly."

DeKok rubbed the bridge of his nose with his little finger.

"Did Abbenes have any clue about the identity of the caller?"

The doctor pulled up his shoulder in an uncharacteristic, baffled gesture.

"Perhaps he did. I do not know. He just said a woman had arranged a meeting at that late hour. He did not reveal the name of the female to me." He gestured apologetically. "And I am a gentleman, after all. I did not inquire."

DeKok merely nodded.

"And if, eh, Mr. Abbenes *had* told you the name of the woman, would you have been forthcoming enough to tell me?"

Hardinxveld grinned suddenly.

"That, my dear inspector, is a hypothetical question. He did not reveal the name to me. If Abbenes knew her, it will forever be his, and her, secret."

DeKok rubbed his face with a flat hand. It was to gain some time. He was looking for a way to steer the interrogation in a new direction.

"It must have shocked you deeply when you heard about the murder of Abbenes, the next day."

"Indeed."

DeKok feigned admiration.

"It was very wise of you not to respond to the same enticement."

The doctor smiled thinly.

"The brutal death of Abbenes seemed an abundant warning."

"Why did you not warn Mr. Darthouse? An assault on him would also have been, how did you say it, *more or less in the realm of expectations?*"

For the first time it looked like Dr. Hardinxveld was not so self-assured. He nervously fidgeted with his necktie.

"Eh, I did not judge that to be a prudent course of action," he said hesitantly.

DeKok looked surprised.

"I don't understand."

Hardinxveld stroked his neck with the tops of his fingers, as if tempted to loosen his collar.

"The phone call I received...I recognized the sexy voice."

"What?"

Dr. Hardinxveld nodded slowly, reluctantly.

"It was Sybille, Darthouse's wife."

16

DeKok drove away from the curb. He was irritated, struggling with his discomfort. The car was in the wrong gear and jumped like a wild bronco. DeKok slammed backward, then forward, until the movement slowed. He hadn't shifted to the right gear; the speed of the vehicle finally matched the gear position. The engine didn't conk out, as it often did when DeKok drove. By his own admission he was probably the worst driver in The Netherlands, possibly all of Europe. It took more than twenty tries to get his driver's license, and the lack of practice had not improved his skills.

He had a deep need to flee the city. He longed to race through Amsterdam and go to Seaside, or some other city on the coast. What he needed was to walk along the beach and let the sea breeze blow the cobwebs off of his brain.

He tried to review the conversation with the supposedly affable Dr. Hardinxveld, promptly running a red light. Surprised by the number of angry horns blowing at him, he parked the VW at the far side of the crossing. The car was half on the sidewalk and crooked. He shut down the engine.

To say that DeKok did not enjoy driving was an understatement. He had been born too late. He would have felt completely at home in the time of horse-drawn stagecoaches, carriages, and canal boats. He believed in walking at a leisurely pace to most destinations.

DeKok soon realized he could not leave the VW with both front wheels on the sidewalk. After several tries he found reverse, almost causing a collision, and reached a parking space. Finally he felt he was completely safe. He switched off the engine again.

It was time to analyze the conversation with the good doctor. What did Hardinxveld really tell him? And what could he concluded from any of it? At least the story was a reasonable explanation for the presence of the doctor's car, engine still warm, at Abbenes' murder scene. It would be easy to confirm Abbenes' car problem, the clogged fuel line that prompted the vehicle exchange.

DeKok leaned back. He felt in his heart Hardinxveld's story would hold up under scrutiny. Hardinxveld wanted him to believe it was no more than a romantic adventure. It didn't ring true.

He wondered whether Abbenes' visit to Hardinxveld served more than one purpose? Was it prompted by a defective fuel line or did Abbenes want to consult with his friend? Did he want to discuss agreements...proposals...goals? If so, Hardinxveld was very much aware of the identity of Abbenes' alleged tryst.

DeKok rubbed his chin. He had been genuinely shocked when Hardinxveld revealed that he, too, had received a late-night invitation to meet on the very spot where Darthouse's murder had taken place. Hardinxveld *must* know something, DeKok had been careful not to identify the exact location. Had there really been an attempt to entice the doctor to that fatal spot? Or did Hardinxveld know about it because he was the murderer?

DeKok sighed deeply. He had seldom dealt with such a miserable case. The stress of it kept intruding on his mind. Hardinxveld was very intelligent. There was no doubt about it. DeKok was certain the doctor had misled him in suggesting Sybille Darthouse was his anonymous caller. He could imagine the attractive woman enticing the lawyer to the murder scene. It was also possible she would try to get Hardinxveld to Wester Church. But the absurdity of the story was the notion Darthouse would have dashed, panting, to an assignation involving his own wife.

Obviously there was no doubt Darthouse had gone to Wester Church and found his death on Wester Market, just behind the church. So, why did Darthouse go out in the middle of the night? What could have been the motive for leaving his comfortable house in Amstelveen? Did the same motive drive Abbenes to his death?

DeKok pulled out his lower lip and let it plop back. There was no one around to censure the disgusting habit, so he plopped away for several minutes, ordering his thoughts. Why did Hardinxveld lie to him? Did the surgeon have a part in the macabre happenings? Was he an accomplice rather than a potential victim? What about the seven iron missing from his golf bag?

DeKok remained seated for awhile. Then he resolutely stepped out of the car and locked it. He hailed a passing cab and took it to Warmoes Street. Somebody else could pick up the car. He was not driving again, not today.

Vledder was the first thing DeKok noticed when he entered the detective room. He was, as usual, behind

his computer. DeKok crossed the room to Vledder's desk
in a few long strides.

"You were supposed to go to bed," growled DeKok.
"We had agreed on that."

The young inspector shook his head.

"I couldn't," he protested. "I was on my way home, but
I couldn't shake the thought of all the things we still have
to do." He took a deep breath. "So I came back."

DeKok smiled. It was not just lack of practice, the
department wasn't dragging him by the hair into the so-
called age of telecommunications. He never even switched
on his computer; as far as he was concerned it could gather
dust on the corner of his desk until he retired.

"How do you feel?"

"Not too bad. I think I'm getting my second wind.
Perhaps we'll be able to go home early tonight."

DeKok grinned.

"Count on it. We'll just let the corpses we discover pile
up until tomorrow."

Vledder laughed.

"We could do that. For sure *they* aren't in a hurry."

DeKok hung up his coat and hat, walked back, and sank
down in a chair in front of Vledder's desk.

"I saw Dr. Hardinxveld this morning…at noon, actually."

Vledder nodded. DeKok restrained him from pulling
his keyboard closer.

"Let that thing wait for awhile."

"All right—did you get any useful information from the
doctor?"

DeKok pushed out his lower lip.

"Among other things he said *he* had received a phone
call asking him to go to Wester Church."

Vledder's eyes widened.

"Where we found the corpse of Darthouse?"

"Exactly."

"Who called him?"

"A woman who didn't identify herself. The doctor thought he recognized her voice."

"Really? That's great!" exclaimed Vledder.

DeKok nodded slowly.

"Sybille, Darthouse's wife."

"I don't believe it."

DeKok shrugged.

"Why not?"

"I can imagine a young, vivacious woman wanting to get rid of her much older husband. But why would she want to kill Abbenes and Hardinxveld?"

DeKok nodded his agreement.

"Fine, she may or may not have had motive to kill her husband. What I cannot imagine is Darthouse excitedly trekking to Wester Church in response to a phone call from his own wife."

Vledder shook his head.

"Not only far-fetched, but it would have been impossible. She was there, in bed, when Darthouse got his call."

DeKok raised an index finger in the air and studied it.

"Careful there," he said after a long pause. "She said she was home and in bed. Outside of her statement, we have no proof." He rubbed the back of his neck. "I've been thinking about it for a long time. By the way, I left the car parked on a street. Couldn't drive it anymore, something wrong with it—"

"Where did you leave it?" interrupted Vledder.

DeKok told him where and Vledder made a note.

"I'll have the garage tow it in."

"No, don't do that. It will probably start up again. Here are the keys."

He tossed the keys on the desk. Vledder looked at him, then smiled to himself. Vledder said nothing; he knew there was nothing wrong with the car, just the driver.

"Well, what did you conclude from the doctor's remarks?" asked Vledder, changing the subject.

"As I said, he gave me food for thought. Do you think it's possible Sybille called her husband from a different location, to ask him to meet at Wester Church? Then, after killing her husband, could have raced back to Amstelveen to be ready for us?"

Vledder grimaced.

"That's rather convoluted, don't you think?" Then his eyes lit up. "It would be different if we could discover a motive for her to kill Abbenes."

"Very good, Dick," said DeKok. "You're shining so brightly why would you need a night's sleep?"

"Spare me," begged Vledder. "I want to *keep* a clear mind."

DeKok smiled and abruptly changed the subject.

"You were at the autopsy?"

"Yes, you know that."

"Of course. Did Dr. Rusteloos find anything interesting, out of the ordinary?"

Vledder shook his head.

"He worked at his usual speed and drew to a quick conclusion. He called Darthouse a copy of Abbenes."

"The murder weapon was a seven iron?"

"Yes. The shape and measurements of the wound were identical to those of Abbenes. Even the spot on the back of the head was almost identical."

"A *modus operandi*," murmured DeKok. "We have one perpetrator."

"I'm convinced of it. Dr. Rusteloos agreed."

"Did he offer anything about time of death?"

"Nothing definite. Death occurred several hours after he had last eaten, was all Rustcloos was willing to state."

"Well, Frankie still has no alibi."

"No," said Vledder, pulling something out of his pocket. It was wrapped in tissue paper. He handed the packet to DeKok. "This was found around his neck."

DeKok unwrapped the item.

"Another bull...a Taurus."

Vledder shook his head.

"And it's wrong again."

"How's that?"

Darthouse was born on April 3. He's no Taurus, he's a Ram, an Aries.

"Well, well. According to Mrs. Abbenes, it is a calf. I don't know what to make of it."

"Me, either," said Vledder.

DeKok took the receiver from Vledder.

"Why do I have to come downstairs?" he asked, irked.

"She came in," answered Meindert Post at the other end of the line. "She told me she wanted to speak to you. But she refused to go upstairs."

"Who?"

"The woman...she's ashamed."

DeKok snorted. The slow progress of the investigation had not improved his disposition.

"She's too ashamed to climb some stairs?"

Meindert's voice came over the line at a fraction of his usual volume.

"Is that so unusual?" he demanded. "Maybe it embarrasses her to be here."

DeKok groaned.

"It could happen."

"Don't be so cynical, DeKok," chided Post over the phone. "The woman doesn't want to be seen in the detective room with all the cops and perps. Show some understanding. She does seem to have something to say of a confidential nature. I have an empty cell for you. Put in a table and two chairs—it will be just like a regular interrogation room."

DeKok looked at the doors of the interrogation rooms. In some cases you had to almost crawl over someone's desk to get in. There was no such thing as discretion. He smiled.

"That's the best you can do?"

"Just come down here," said Meindert Post, "or I'll come and get you." He broke the connection.

DeKok went downstairs. He walked up behind Post and tapped him on the shoulder.

"Where is she?" he asked gently.

The watch commander went to the door that led to the cells, opened it, and led the inspector down the stairs. There were twelve cells down here, six on each side of a dimly lit corridor. Only two doors were closed and locked. The other doors stood open.

"Just a couple of drunks who haven't been picked up yet," said Meindert, indicating the locked doors.

He stopped in front of the open door of the last cell in the row. He gestured toward the table.

"Call me when you're through."

DeKok nodded and entered the cell.

Behind a table was a young woman of about twenty-seven, maybe twenty-eight years. She had beautiful, long, blonde hair and a magnificent, barely concealed, bosom. She rose and hesitantly stretched out her hand.

"I'm Sophie, Sophie Peters."

DeKok took the offered hand.

"Frankie Kraay's ex-wife?" he asked suspiciously.

She sat down.

"You can forget the 'ex' pretty soon."

"Why, you're officially divorced, aren't you?"

She nodded slowly.

"Believe me, it still hurts inside. I love the guy."

DeKok was speechless.

"He said you were unfaithful to him. Did he not find you in bed with someone else?"

She shook her head sadly.

"It wasn't unfaithfulness. I did not cheat."

DeKok grinned, still puzzled.

"What would you call it?"

Sophie looked at him with big, sad eyes.

"They say you're a man with a lot of life experience, someone with understanding. That is why I came."

DeKok raised his arms in surrender.

"All right, Sophie. I'll listen."

She lowered her head, avoiding his eyes.

"Before I met Frankie I was in *the life.*"

"Did Frankie know that?"

She shook her head.

"Men are often just children. Some thoughts they can't stand."

"And Frankie is one of them?"

A tender smile made her face radiant.

"Frankie is a big man," she said with a thrill in her voice. "He's a wonderful, loving, strong, foolish man-child. The moment I saw him, I knew I was lost."

"So you got married?"

Her face fell.

"After the honeymoon the trouble started. Frankie worked sunup to sundown every day. If everything went smoothly, he brought in a few hundred a week. He had so many worries. There were unpaid bills, demanding suppliers, customers who paid late or not at all." She paused and chewed on a cuticle. "Believe this, whores earn a lot of money. I had some annoying clients, but on the whole, it was easy money. When I saw Frankie fight and struggle for every penny, I hurt for him." She pressed a hand to her ample chest, "Here."

DeKok understood.

"And you decided to help Frankie your way?"

Tears came into her eyes.

"When he caught me, there was no time to explain. He wouldn't listen. He chased me out of the house and a few days later his lawyer, Abbenes, was after me."

DeKok rubbed his nose with his little finger.

"But, eh, Abbenes came up with some extremely favorable conditions for you in the divorce settlement. Rumor has it your, as one says, personal charms had something to do with that."

She raked her fingers though her hair.

"Abbenes wasn't the kind of man to fall for a woman of my type."

DeKok looked puzzled.

"Not your type?" he reacted spontaneously. "I think you're a positively delectable woman. I wouldn't be the only one to feel that way, I think."

Sophie gave him a sweet smile.

"You are not Abbenes. He was absolutely not charmed by young, self-confident women."

"No?"

She shook her head resolutely.

"He preferred children."

"Children?" DeKok was disgusted.

She nervously picked at an invisible thread on her sleeve.

"He went for little girls, the younger the better, preferably without experience."

DeKok narrowed his eyes.

"He told you that?"

Sophie Peters shook her head.

"He didn't have to," she said with a grimace. "Once I'm alone with a man for a few minutes, I know all I need to know."

DeKok loosened his collar. "An enviable gift," he said hoarsely. "But where it concerns women, I lack the gift. I still don't understand why you wanted to see me."

She looked at him. Her face was expressionless.

"Frankie is with me."

When DeKok returned to the detective room, he found Vledder with his head in his hands. The gray sleuth tapped him on the shoulder.

"What's the matter?" he asked, worried.

Vledder pointed an index finger at a memo pad.

"I just received word from St. Matthew's Hospital."
DeKok felt the tension in his chest.
"Dr. Hardinxveld?"
The young man nodded.
"He died from a single blow to the back of the skull."

17

Vledder parked the marked patrol car in the parking lot. Two uniformed constables were unceremoniously evicted from the vehicle and dispatched to pick up the team's battered and abandoned vehicle. The constables were to bring the VW back, and then leave with the patrol car. Despite DeKok's repeated assurances that "the gears don't work," the desk cancelled the tow truck.

As they exited the car, they stretched.

"I hope we soon have our own car back," said DeKok.

"I thought you didn't care for cars."

"I don't, but this car is worse." He kicked the tires. "How can a sane person think in it? There are two radios, a computer, a location thingamajig, not to mention, other gadgetry! It's too much."

Vledder smiled, he secretly agreed that a GPS in an Amsterdam patrol car was superfluous, to say the least. But he heartily appreciated all the other electronic systems incorporated in the vehicle.

"Inspector, had you not broken our regular VW, you wouldn't have to put up with all this stuff."

DeKok growled something unintelligible.

They looked up at the facade of the enormous St. Matthew's Hospital. Vledder was impressed, but DeKok was not pleased with the vista. It was modern, too cubist for his taste.

He found all the steel and glass impersonal. The intimate, spread-out buildings of the old Welhelmina Hospital, almost hidden by trees and greenery, were more to his taste.

In the vast lobby, soft conversation mingled to form an anxious hum. An older nurse walked toward them. She looked at the senior partner.

"You're Inspector DeKok?"

He nodded.

"With a kay-oh-kay," he said automatically. "This is my colleague, Inspector Dick Vledder."

The nurse searched their faces with an appraising look. It took seconds, but both men felt she had seen everything she needed to see.

"I'm Chief Nurse Westerveld," she said abruptly. "Please follow me."

They followed her to a large alcove on the side of the entrance hall. Elevator doors lined three walls of the alcove. She walked to one of the elevators and pushed a button.

"We can't go all the way by elevator," she explained. "The last stretch we'll have to climb the stairs."

The elevator door opened and they stepped inside. Nurse Westerveld pushed another button and the elevator shot up with nauseating speed.

DeKok leaned over.

"Did you find him?"

She shook her head.

"It was Theresa, a girl from administration. The child was so upset, I sent her home," she said in a tone that smothered any disagreement with her actions.

DeKok looked at her with a bland face.

"The girl works in administration here?" he asked, baffled.

The nurse pointed up.

"Practically nobody goes to that space. It contains only file cabinets. Administration uses it as storage space."

"And that's where the body is?"

"Yes," she answered sharply. "That's where he is. They told us not to touch or move anything. Besides, any idiot could see there was nothing else to do."

"Quite right," said DeKok. "How did Dr. Hardinxveld get to be there?"

"Who knows? It's a mystery to us. Dr. Hardinxveld belongs in surgery. He would have no business there."

The elevator stopped. The doors opened onto a long, deserted corridor.

Nurse Westerveld again preceded them. At the end of the corridor she opened a door. There was a small landing, at the end of which was a rather steep, iron staircase.

DeKok pointed at the door.

"Is that ever locked?"

"No, why?"

DeKok did not answer. He entered the door and climbed the steel staircase. Vledder and the chief nurse followed.

They arrived in a large, low space without windows. A few fluorescent lights were mounted on the steel beams of the ceiling. They shed an eerie light on the silent file cabinets along the walls. At the end was a wide door.

Almost in the middle of the space a man in a white coat was supine on the concrete floor. DeKok looked down at him. He recognized him immediately. Only this morning those eyes had looked at the world cheerily, almost amused. Now vacant, they reflected only death. Around the head was a circle of coagulated blood. Blood also stuck to the back of his head.

DeKok kneeled next to the victim. Suddenly he jumped up, as if stung by a bee. An overpowering noise filled the low space. He looked around wildly. He saw the nurse's lips moving, but could not hear her. After awhile, the noise lessened, until it died away altogether. It was replaced with the whine of a large elevator. A light flashed by at the end of the space, behind the large door.

"What the—" he exclaimed.

"It was a helicopter," explained the nurse calmly. "We're underneath the heliport on the roof. This space not only strengthens the roof, it acts as a sound barrier between the hospital proper—it is an addition."

"But I heard an elevator pass," said Vledder.

"Yes," she responded, unruffled. "One large elevator serves the heliport. It is for patients and staff who travel to and from the heliport. It's not for just anyone," she added primly.

"I see," said DeKok, dismissing the subject. He had seen a gleaming round object behind the right shoulder of the corpse. He bent to pick it up, and put it in his pocket.

"What is it?" asked Vledder.

"A two-Euro coin somebody must have lost." He straightened out. His knees creaked. "Did you alert the herd?"

"Yes, from the car. Didn't you hear me?"

"I wasn't listening—thought you were just playing with your new toys."

Vledder started to grin, but then he pointed over DeKok's shoulder. DeKok turned around and saw Dr. Koning, the old, eccentric coroner, approach. Two morgue attendants, carrying the ubiquitous stretcher, followed on his heels.

When the aged coroner reached DeKok, they shook hands formally. Then the coroner took off his old, greenish Garibaldi hat and knelt down next to the corpse. He moved the head slightly to get a better look at the wound. Then he closed the eyes of the corpse.

"Another upstanding member of our community," said DeKok.

Dr. Koning looked up.

"Our oh-so-reliable Grim Reaper does not take into account his clients' social status."

DeKok nodded.

"Neither does my murderer."

Koning stretched out a hand and DeKok hastened to help him stand up. With precise movements, he took out a large, white handkerchief from the breast pocket of his coat. Next he took off his pince-nez and started an elaborate cleaning process. Finally he replaced the glasses on his nose and replaced the handkerchief in the pocket of his old-fashioned tailcoat.

"All these heavy blunt-force traumas," he said in a scratchy voice. "It looks like an epidemic. If I were you, DeKok, I'd tell your future victims to wear hard hats."

"I would, if I could," answered DeKok. "Ironically, this is the second man who had every opportunity to tell me he was threatened, and refused to ask for protection."

"I didn't see the first one, but I heard about it, of course. From what I hear, however, neither this one nor the two previous cases are exactly a great loss."

"Doctor," said DeKok, shocked. "I've never heard you say such a thing."

"You didn't this time, either," replied the coroner. "By the way," he added, "he is officially dead."

DeKok nodded.

"I knew that...killed with a seven iron."

The next morning DeKok was early getting to the station house. The murder of Dr. Hardinxveld had not succeeded in pushing him deeper into the quagmire this case presented. On the contrary, he had a distinct feeling the framework of his theory was taking shape, solidifying. He had a clear shot at a solution. Of one thing he was certain: he had to find the killer before the next victim surfaced.

He took a blank sheet of paper out of a drawer. He drew some lines on it, dividing it into columns. Then he started to fill in the spaces between the lines. He put all the known facts about each victim in a separate column. He also prepared a column for Frankie and each witness. Before he wrote anything down, however, he realized that Vledder could give him all of it in a few minutes of keyboard strokes. He crumpled the paper in a ball and tossed it in the wastebasket.

His old friend, Adjutant Kamphouse, came into the room and walked over to DeKok's desk.

"I've bad news for you."

"Oh, I'm getting early retirement?"

Kamphouse laughed.

"You can forget that. For the time being they can't do without you." He became more serious. "Vledder called in sick, this morning. He was very upset about it. I was asked to tell you that he's sorry, but he's completely laid-up."

DeKok looked distressed.

"I was afraid this would happen. The boy has hardly slept at all for several days. Sooner or later we all pay the piper." He looked up at Kamphouse. "I need some freedom of movement for the immediate future. Do you have someone who can go to the autopsy for me? It's at ten o'clock, at the lab."

The adjutant nodded.

"I'll send Ans. She's good. Is there anything specific she should look for?"

"A woman?" queried DeKok. "I didn't think alot of women worked homicide."

"Be careful, DeKok. You're dating yourself. Anyway, it wasn't a lateral move. She transferred as a detective. Actually, I think you know her. She's worked with us before."

"She has?"

DeKok thought.

"No," he said after awhile. "The only Ans I remember is a constable. She helped us out by impersonating a prostitute so we could catch a murderer."

"That's her, but a constable no longer. Ans Rozier is now a detective-sergeant—she's been working plain-clothes at headquarters for the last two years."

"Well, well," said DeKok. "How time flies. Yes," he then decided, "Ans will do very well. I hope she has attended at least one autopsy before."

"Don't worry about that. It was part of her training. Well, anything particular she should be looking for, or asking?"

DeKok nodded slowly to himself. He visualized the constable he had known—a petite, athletic blonde with an elfin face.

"Yes," he said. "Have her contact Weelen. I want accurate, detailed close-ups of the wound. Also, I want the little bull."

"What little bull?"

DeKok gave him a wan smile.

"I'm convinced that Hardinxveld has a little bull on a chain around his neck."

"Like a zodiac sign? Is the man a Taurus?"

DeKok shook his head.

"No, he's a Leo, and it isn't a bull, but a calf."

DeKok requested and received a bicycle from the watch commander. It was the typical police bicycle, black, upright, without speed gears, the top of the rear wheel and the drive chain neatly enclosed in gleaming vinyl. DeKok remembered when all police constables patrolled on bicycles. They patrolled the city in pairs on shiny black bicycles, stiffly upright, in immaculate uniforms. Any disturbance would immediately subside when they turned a corner. Sometimes they would walk the bicycle and sometimes they would lean it against a lamp post and chat with people in the neighborhoods. Strange, thought DeKok, police officers seemed to be more respected when they patrolled on foot, or on a bicycle. Was that because they were closer to the people in the city? Nowadays, most officers roar around in closed cars. You sometimes can not even see the faces. It had all become so impersonal and the crime rate was increasing steadily.

There had to be a lesson there, mused DeKok, as he steadily peddled along. He passed the Royal Palace, driving along Nicholas Street, until he turned a familiar corner. He found himself in front of number 876. He leaned the bicycle against a convenient lamp post and secured it.

He walked over to the door and rang the doorbell.

It took a few minutes for Casper Hoogwoud to open the door. The young man looked neglected. He had a three-day stubble, and his hair hung down in strings. He tightened the cord of his dressing gown with an angry gesture. He gave DeKok a challenging look.

Without saying a word, DeKok pushed the young man aside and entered the residence. He walked directly through the corridor to the living room. When Casper hastened after him, he turned around and took the young man by the shoulders and pushed him forcefully into a chair. The old sleuth loomed threateningly over him.

"Now I want the truth about the money."

"What money?"

"The hundred thousand you wore on your belly the day Marcel died."

Casper tried a weak defense.

"I told you, I withdrew it from my account at the Ijsselstein Bank."

DeKok narrowed his eyes and his face looked menacing.

"You never had an account with that bank."

A spark of the previous defiance returned. "Says who?"

"Mr. Darthouse, the managing director of the bank."

Casper made a defeated gesture.

"Okay, the account wasn't in my name. The account was in Marcel's name."

"And there was a hundred thousand in that account?"

Casper Hoogwoud smirked.

"There was a lot more, at times. Sometimes as much as half a million. Marcel was so sick toward the end, he wasn't able to get the money from the bank himself."

"And that's why you did it?"

"Yes."

"With an authorization from Marcel?"

Casper shook his head.

"Marcel never wanted to give me authorization."

"Why not?"

"He didn't want anybody to know he was sick."

DeKok was perplexed.

"How did you manage it?"

"Marcel and I looked alike. If I dressed like him, combed my hair the same way, most people couldn't tell the difference."

"So, you presented yourself at the bank as Marcel Hoogwoud."

"Right."

"And Marcel knew that?"

Casper nodded with animation.

"Of course Marcel knew that," he reacted sharply. "Do you think I played that masquerade on my own? I had to do it. Marcel asked me to."

"And the money you got from the bank in this manner, you gave to Marcel?"

"Yes."

"Except for that hundred thousand."

Casper sighed.

"That was the last of the money in the account. Marcel told me to keep it for myself in case something happened to him. It would give me a little nest egg, a new start for me. Marcel also advised me *not* to put it in a bank."

"Why not?"

"He said nobody, not the government nor the police, could confiscate it."

DeKok was tired of standing up. It was no longer neces-sary to intimidate Casper. With a relieved sigh he sat down in the easy chair across from the young man.

"Why would Abbenes accuse you of fraud?"

Casper smiled crookedly.

"They figured out, somehow, that I had been taking the money out of Marcel's account. They wanted that money back."

"Who are *they*?"

"The people from the bank, the Ijsselstein Bank...they had hired Abbenes to put pressure on me. If I didn't return the money, they would sue. Accuse me, take me to court. According to Abbenes, I had deliberately swindled the bank. He said he could also get me on falsification of documents and impersonating a depositor. Not only had I pretended to be my brother, I had forged his signature."

DeKok was curious.

"Weren't you afraid Abbenes would actually take you to court, not just threaten?"

Casper grinned with gleaming eyes.

"When I told Marcel what Abbenes said, he told me not to worry. He started to laugh out loud, as a matter of fact. 'Let them threaten,' he said. 'They don't have enough guts to come after you.'"

DeKok rubbed his chin pensively.

"Marcel was convinced?" he asked, disbelieving.

"Absolutely."

"How did Marcel get the money in the first place, at least half a million, you said?"

Casper shrugged nonchalantly.

"Marcel often traveled abroad, by himself, on business."

"What kind of business?"

The young man threw both arms above his head.

"I don't know that. Really, I don't. Marcel never talked

about it to me."

"Then, who knows?"

"I think my father knows."

"What do you mean you think?"

Casper avoided DeKok's eyes while he talked.

"Once when I was alone with my father at Amstel Land, he said to me, 'Your brother, Marcel, is a real smart fellow. He'll get them.'"

DeKok gave the young man a searching look.

"Did you understand what your father meant?"

The young man shook his head.

"That's why I asked how Marcel got so smart."

"And?"

"My father ignored the question and changed the subject."

DeKok nodded to himself.

"And now Marcel is dead."

Casper lowered his head.

"I buried him yesterday."

18

Jaap Groen approached DeKok with outstretched arms and a broad smile on his face.

"My very good friend," he said with feeling. "Welcome, welcome to my humble abode. What a surprise and what a joy to be able to greet you."

DeKok blushed under the extravagant reception. He had known the famed Amsterdam historian and theologian since middle school, when they had organized clubs and tried to discover the mysteries of female pulchritude.

After mutual hugs, Jaap Groen led the way to a comfortably furnished living room and pointed at an easy chair.

"Sit down, sit you down," he said busily. "Tell me what I can do for you."

DeKok obliged and placed his hat on the floor next to the chair.

"I want to call on your knowledge of the Bible."

Groen clasped his hand in front of him.

"It will be an honor and a blessing," he exclaimed joyously, "to explain God's word to you."

DeKok smiled.

"I am in charge," he said, all businesslike, "of investigating a series of gruesome murders. There have been three installments so far. Dead, in order, are a lawyer, a bank director, and a surgeon from St. Matthew's Hospital.

All three died due to severe blows to the head with a seven iron, a golf club. There are such remarkable coincidences surrounding these murders, I'm convinced the same person committed all three. The *modus operandi* leaves no other conclusion."

Jaap Groen raised his arms in a theatrical gesture.

"And outside," he declared enthusiastically, "are the dogs, the whore mongers, and the slayers, the priests of false gods and all who worship the lie and act accordingly." With a deep sigh he lowered his arms. "And you, my dear friend, walk in a dark cloud of sin and seek the light."

The gray sleuth resisted the urge to applaud and cry "Bravo!" Respect for his friend restrained him. He knew from experience that Jaap Groen usually meant every word he said.

"After the murder of the lawyer," continued DeKok, "our commissaris received a phone call. It was a terse sentence: *'Abbenes,'* that was the name of the lawyer, *'Abbenes is dead, not because of your righteousness, but because of mine.'* After the other murders he received similar calls, with the exception of the name. The name changed with the victim.

"Extraordinary."

DeKok nodded agreement and continued his story.

"That text intrigues me greatly. I have the feeling those words, apart from their literal meaning, contain a message, a pointer. That is why it may be a Bible text, one of those texts that requires a special explanation."

"An exegesis," said Groen with a calm, serious face.

"Exactly."

The theologian sank deep in thought.

"In Deuteronomy," he declared, after a long pause, "Chapter Nine, Verse Six, God states, through Moses, that he will keep his promise to the people of Israel. But he cautions, '…not because of your righteousness.' God then expresses wrath over their obstinate persistence in sin. The Israelites had built a golden calf, had danced around this golden calf and had worshipped it."

DeKok looked up.

"A golden calf," he repeated tonelessly.

"The golden calf," explained Groen, "was in fact a young bull. In a number of cultures and eras it was a symbol of life, power, and, above all, a symbol of sex."

DeKok looked at his friend with admiration.

"Sex," he repeated pensively. "Sex, of course, that's it!" He thought for awhile before he asked his next question.

"Who, eh, who would you expect to know the connection between the text, 'not because of your righteousness,' and a young bull symbolizing sex?"

Jaap Groen reflected.

"There are," he said slowly, "simple believers who enjoy the privilege of understanding God's word without explanation. They do not need an exegesis." He hesitated a moment. "But, yet, in this context, I would be inclined to think first of a Bible scholar, or a cleric…a priest, a minister, a rabbi."

DeKok understood. He stood up, grabbing his hat from the floor as he did so. He shook hands with the scholar.

"You've been a tremendous help," he said gratefully. "It gives me a direction to take." He moved toward the door, then turned around.

"What happened to the golden calf?"

Groen raised both arms as if in supplication.

"Moses spoke to the people of Israel, saying, 'And I took your sin, the calf which ye had made, and burned it with fire, and stamped it, and ground it very small, even until it was as small as dust; and I cast the dust thereof into the brook that descended out of the mount.'"

DeKok nodded to himself.

"He performed a rather radical destruction."

Jaap Groen smiled and placed a hand on his friend's shoulder.

"Moses was an impulsive man."

Contentedly DeKok peddled his bicycle through the city. He observed all traffic regulations and missed not a single stop sign. Yet he had time to reflect on what he had learned. Like most Dutch people, DeKok was completely at home on a bicycle. Even today, with the proliferation of motorized transport, there are still about 10 million bicycles in The Netherlands, serving a population of around 15 million. Bike traffic is as strictly regulated as all other traffic. It is even possible to get a speeding ticket on a bicycle. Dutch bicyclists wouldn't dream of riding their bikes the wrong way on a one-way street, nor would they run a red light.

In a car, DeKok had endless problems with the car itself, the traffic, and the traffic regulations. On a bicycle, he sailed majestically through traffic, without giving it a second thought.

The revelation of the golden calf as a young bull had sped up his thought processes. Had the widow of Abbenes tried to steer (he smiled at the unintended pun) his investigation in the right direction with her postscript at the bottom of her inexplicable note? What direction? Did she know the connection between the murderer and the golden calf around her husband's neck?

The biblical calf had been thoroughly destroyed by Moses. Did that mean a biblical condemnation of sex? Was the message that even the symbol of sex had to be ground into dust? Who thought that way? And who would be prepared to commit a series of murders because of that conviction?

In front of the church, he leaned the bike against the wall and secured it. Then he approached the door of the vicarage and rang the doorbell.

The wide, dark green door was opened by a dignified man in a black suit. He looked to be about fifty years old. The man had a long face, white as wax, and wavy, gray hair. His pale blue eyes were enlarged by a pair of thick glasses in dark brown frames.

"Yes?" he asked haughtily.

DeKok lifted his decrepit little hat and held it in front of his chest.

"My name is DeKok," he said amicably, "with a kay-oh-kay. I'm a police inspector attached to Warmoes Street Station. I would like to talk with you." He held his head to one side and smiled. "You are, I take it, Mr. Leem?"

The man nodded.

"I am, yes." He adjusted his glasses. "About what did you want to talk?"

DeKok studied his waxen pallor and arrogant expression.

"The golden calf."

A sudden tic developed on Leem's left cheek.

"Come again?" he asked, suspicion in his tone.

DeKok nodded.

"It seems an interesting subject."

Mr. Leem opened wider the green door and indicated

DeKok could come in. Leem led the way across a red-tiled floor to a small, oak-paneled room. Under a tall window stood a rough-hewn table, flanked by two leather chairs.

After they entered, Leem closed the door and locked it. He put the key in his pocket of his jacket.

DeKok held up his outstretched hand, palm up.

"You may as well give me the key."

Leem smiled.

"I just want to make sure we're not disturbed."

DeKok kept his hand extended.

"The key," he insisted. "I'd like to have a path of retreat, in case you have a golf club around somewhere."

The minister looked scared from behind his thick glasses. Slowly he felt in his pocket and placed the key carefully in DeKok's open palm.

"If it makes you happy," he said, with a slight quaver in his voice.

DeKok's face remained a steel mask.

"And now give me the golf club."

Leem shrugged his shoulders.

"What golf club?"

"The seven iron."

"What seven iron?"

DeKok looked at him evenly.

"I refer to the golf club used to kill Attorney Abbenes, Bank Director Darthouse, and Doctor Hardinxveld."

Leem was visibly nervous.

"What do those murders have to do with me?"

DeKok brought his face closer to that of the minister.

"Don't you belong to the 'Four-Leaf Clover,' also called the 'Clover Quartet' or, in whispers, the 'Sex Quartet?'"

Leem swallowed.

"I am, as are—were—the men you mentioned, a member of the golf club, Amstel Land. I have nothing else in common with them."

With lightning movement, DeKok placed his flat hand on the chest of the man in front of him. Under his shirt he felt a small chain with the pendant of a small animal. He knew exactly what kind of animal that was.

With a malicious grin, he pointed at the rough-hewn table and the two flanking chairs.

"Well, Shepherd of Souls, it is confession time."

19

DeKok gave his young colleague a friendly smile.

"How are you feeling?" he asked, concern in his eyes.

"Not too bad, considering. I just couldn't stay home any longer." He grinned. "For awhile I was in bad shape—a bug, maybe. My head felt like it was full of holes. I must have slept about twenty hours in one stretch."

"Well, in that case, you're through sleeping, aren't you? I mean you had enough."

"Yes. But that doesn't mean I want to work through the night again...at least not for awhile."

"Anyway, while you were gone, I made some discoveries that made me pretty hopeful. For one thing, I visited my old friend Jaap Groen and—"

He did not complete the sentence, but stared away into the distance. Suddenly he took his feet off the desk, stood up, and walked over to Vledder's desk. He placed a hand on the shoulder of the young man.

"Dick," he said, his voice tinged with sentiment, "you have always been a good partner and a fine colleague, a friend. Even when you did not agree with me, you always stood by me. You've done the same in this case. I'm very grateful."

Vledder grimaced.

"Don't be so melodramatic."

DeKok shook his head.

"I mean it, Dick. That's why I hope to be able to count on you again."

"Of course you can count on me," Vledder said with conviction.

DeKok walked back to his own desk and leaned on a corner.

"Fine, then that is settled."

Vledder looked at his mentor with growing suspicion.

"Are you planning something?"

DeKok nodded slowly.

"I'm going to disappear for a day, maybe two days, but definitely not longer. If the commissaris or the judge advocate ask for me, make up something." A smile played around his lips. "Please don't worry about a thing. I will contact you before the finale."

"What do you mean, 'finale?'"

DeKok chewed on his lower lip.

"I think I'm close."

The young inspector looked apprehensive.

"What are you going to do?"

DeKok ignored the tone of anxiety in his colleague's voice.

"Something for which I can't have any witnesses.

"And what is that?"

"I'm going to arrange a murder."

Exactly fifteen hours later, at a quarter to one in the morning, DeKok returned to the detective room. He seemed strained and under tension. Quickly he walked over to Vledder.

"Has anyone asked for me?"

Vledder shook his head.

"Just Little Lowee called. I think I understood him. He knows the whereabouts of Frankie."

DeKok nodded vaguely. He did not seem interested.

"Have you enough people?"

Vledder nodded enthusiastically.

"I have Ans Rozier. You remember her? She attended the autopsy for us. Hardinxveld, too, had a little bull on a chain."

"I knew that."

Vledder looked surprised.

"You *knew*?"

DeKok nodded, his mind on other things.

"The little bull is some sort of symbol regarding a shared interest," he explained hastily.

Vledder cocked his head.

"What shared interest?"

DeKok ignored him.

"Who else have we got?"

"In addition to Ans, we have Appie Keizer, Fred Prins, and Johnny Ebersen…and Buitendam."

"Buitendam?"

"We're tapping his phone."

"Why?"

Vledder snorted.

"You remember the woman with the strange phone calls?"

"She won't call this time," said DeKok with certainty.

Vledder was both curious and irritated by his partner's behavior, but fearing a rebuff, he did not ask further.

"Do you think we have enough people?"

DeKok pursed his lips and nodded.

"With the six of us, we'll manage."

"What time is it going to be?"

"The usual time, two o'clock."

"Where?"

"Behind Wester Church again."

Vledder could not contain his curiosity.

"How do you know so much?"

DeKok waved vaguely, ignoring the question. He stood up and ambled over to get his hat and coat. With his hat on the back of his head, he turned around.

"Where are the others?"

"In the kitchen, drinking coffee."

"Ask the committee to get ready."

"The committee?"

DeKok grinned. There was a devilish light in his eyes.

"The *Murder Reception Committee.*"

DeKok slid down in the seat. There was no tension now, no anxiety about possible failure. He was convinced those involved would keep their promises, adhere to the plan. There was so much at stake.

He glanced aside at Vledder. The young man leaned forward, both arms on the steering wheel. DeKok understood the dissatisfied look on Vledder's face. But he had been deliberately secretive. Why share the responsibility and *risk* with his colleague? It was he, DeKok, who wanted to shoulder this one. A tired smile played around his lips. How long had he trespassed in the world of crime? How many secrets did he carry in his heart? Truly, his friend Jaap Groen had been right when he said DeKok walked in a dark cloud of sin and sought the light.

He felt Vledder's body suddenly tense. He pushed himself upward and peered over the dashboard. To the left, a man stepped out of a parked car. Limping, one leg dragging behind, he walked slowly toward Wester Church and disappeared in the shadow of a buttress.

Vledder nudged his partner.

"Did you see him?" he panted.

DeKok nodded.

"Did you recognize him?"

"No."

DeKok pointed at the other heavy buttresses of the old church.

"Are the others close enough?" he asked in a whisper. "They must be able to intervene immediately. I wouldn't like to see a real murder committed right before my very own eyes."

Vledder grinned.

"You're the one who wanted to arrange a murder. But don't worry," he said, as he pointed at a lithe female figure slinking from one shadow to another, "the guys are in the right place and Ans just re-positioned herself to get closer."

DeKok took a deep breath.

"You're right," he sighed. "I wanted to arrange a murder, but in full view of reliable witnesses."

"What witnesses?"

DeKok sank back down in the seat.

"You, me, the others. Everything reported in immaculate prose by a half dozen experienced, trustworthy detectives."

Vledder took his arms off the steering wheel.

"We'd appear before the court as material witnesses?"

"Yes."

"What could we establish?"

DeKok waved nonchalantly.

"You will see. We will testify to murder, multiple murders with a golf club, a seven iron to be specific."

Vledder swallowed.

"Where's our murderer?"

"He's there and is cooperating."

"He'll provide evidence against himself?"

"Right."

"Voluntarily?"

DeKok pursed his lips for a moment.

"More or less...yes, you could say that."

Vledder looked at him with disbelieving eyes.

"DeKok," he said, shaking his head, "sometimes you have a bit of the devil in you."

DeKok smiled, flattered.

"The devil, Dick, is a fallen angel."

When the heavy bells of Wester Tower sounded two o'clock, DeKok, again, pressed himself to a more upright position. He realized how extremely important the next few minutes would be. If the actors in the arranged drama did not keep exactly to the script, he could kiss his career goodbye forever. No seniority or past achievements could save him. He'd be retired early and, worse, dishonorably. If he was lucky, he silently admonished himself, it wouldn't be worse.

From the right, from the direction of Princes Canal, a tall, slender figure appeared, dressed in black. When he passed a light post, the glow lit up his long, gray hair. Slowly, hesitantly, as if aware of a looming danger, he walked on.

When the man reached the buttress, DeKok noticed his own respiration become more rapid and he felt the blood rush through his arteries.

Suddenly, the limping man appeared from the shadow. A golf club hung from his right hand. Silently menacing, he approached the tall man. The distance that separated them became smaller.

DeKok jumped out of the car, but Vledder was faster. The young inspector ran ahead of DeKok. Fred Prins and Appie Keizer converged from across the square. Johnny Ebersen emerged from the shadow of a buttress. But it was a lithe, athletic female figure who darted in front of all of them.

The assailant lifted his golf club above his head to administer the fatal blow. Ans Rozier tackled him like a line backer, bringing him down with a thud. Seconds later, when Vledder arrived, she had already turned the man on his stomach and was clasping the handcuffs. With a mischievous grin on her elfin face, she kneeled up and looked at the other police officers.

"We've got him," she said.

"You got him," panted DeKok, who had been outrun by his younger colleagues. "Well, done, my dear."

"That's sergeant to you, inspector," she said severely, but smiled disarmingly as she said it.

Meanwhile, Vledder turned the man on his back. He was preparing to assist him to his feet, when he took a good look at the assailant's face.

"It's Father Hoogwoud."

DeKok nodded complacently.

20

DeKok leaned comfortably back in his easy chair. He felt satisfied and relaxed. He looked at his two visitors.

"The others could not make it?"

Vledder shook his head.

"They would have liked to, but the adjutant needed them for a raid on a fence. Apparently this guy has been buying stolen property from addicts for years. Only Ans," he nodded at his companion, "was able to break away."

"And no less welcome," assured DeKok.

He leaned over and picked up a bottle of cognac from the table next to him. A tray with snifters was already on the table and he poured out two glasses.

"Or would you rather have sherry, sergeant?" he asked with a twinkle in his eye.

"No, thank you, sir. I prefer cognac. And please, call me Ans."

"I will," said DeKok, filling the third snifter, "but you must call me DeKok. I think I told you once before, some time ago, that I'm not a *sir*, just DeKok."

"Yes, you did," Ans replied, remembering. "And I'm sorry, it will not happen again, DeKok."

"Better."

He handed the glasses to his visitors and lifted one for himself.

"To crime," he mocked.

Mrs. DeKok entered and brought a large platter of delicacies. The Dutch seldom drink without eating. And Mrs. DeKok's selection of cocktail food, Vledder knew, was one of the best in the city. She placed the platter in the center of the coffee table and went over to the sideboard to pour herself a glass of sherry. Then she sat down in an easy chair next to her husband.

"Did that man confess?" asked Ans.

"Yes, he did. Father Hoogwoud, or *Dad* as they called him at the golf club, seemed relieved to have it all behind him. He made a full confession. He admitted killing Abbenes, Darthouse, and Hardinxveld. He declared that, but for our intervention, he would have killed Leem as well."

Vledder grinned.

"Exactly in accordance with our official observations."

"Exactly, although I thought for a moment Ans had spoiled it." Before the woman could protest, he hastily continued. "But all's well that ends well. If she had not intervened as quickly as she did, Leem might not have been killed, but he would certainly have been hurt. Also," he continued with a smile at the female officer, "there's no reason why she cannot be a witness, as well as the arresting officer."

"Really?" asked Ans in surprise.

"Yes, that's how it is in the record. You made the arrest, assisted by the rest of us, and we're all witnesses."

The young woman blushed with pleasure. It made her even more attractive. Mrs. DeKok noticed Vledder's sudden interest, but kept silent.

"But why," exclaimed Vledder, "did that old man want to kill those three men, one by one?"

DeKok took a careful sip from his glass and then put it down on the coffee table in front of him. He reached for a cheese croquet, but his wife intervened.

"Jurriaan," she said warningly.

Like a little boy caught with his hand in the cookie jar, DeKok pulled back his hand and sat back.

"To understand it all in full," he began, "we have to travel back in time. Old man Hoogwoud and his three children lived in the greenskeeper's house on the terrain of Amstel Land. It is not surprising the children came into contact with the members of the golf club. Marcel, who played a good game of golf, was very much liked. As Marcel grew up and compared the wealth of the members with the sparse conditions at home, he announced to all who wanted to hear that he intended to become rich quickly. He declared he did not care what he had to do to achieve his goal."

"Even crime," said Vledder.

DeKok smiled.

"He probably did not spell it out, but it must have been clear to everyone he was not rejecting crime as a possibility. Sure enough Abbenes, the lawyer, approached him one day. After a friendly little chat about, eh, sexual pleasures, the lawyer told Marcel he and his friends were charmed by very young girls, preferably exotic girls. He let Marcel know they were prepared to bear whatever costs to indulge in their preferences."

Ans looked disgusted.

"Child prostitution," she said, wrinkling her nose.

"I know how you feel, my dear," said Mrs. DeKok. "I had to swallow hard when I first heard it."

"That is what it was, alright," agreed DeKok.

"Marcel was willing to help?" asked Vledder.

DeKok nodded and took another sip of cognac.

"With money provided by Abbenes, Marcel took a couple of trips to Sri Lanka and Thailand. Within a few months he organized an efficient people-smuggling organization. It worked perfectly. The girls were between twelve and fourteen years old. For a short time, each child was cherished by the members of the Sex Quartet. As they grew older, they disappeared into brothels all over Europe."

Vledder breathed deeply, his drink forgotten.

"Bah," said Ans and drained her glass with one swallow.

"So, that's how Marcel made his money," said Vledder, who was prone to state the obvious.

"The gentlemen," DeKok went on, "wore miniature golden calves around their necks as a sign of their virility."

"Damned bastards," muttered Ans, who was not aware of DeKok's aversion to strong language. But it sounded heartfelt.

DeKok glanced at her for a moment, but said nothing. He knew exactly how the young woman felt.

"Anyway," resumed DeKok, "Marcel arranged the logistics, so gentlemen could have their sex parties. During one of those orgies, Marcel photographed the men in extremely compromising situations."

Vledder looked surprised.

"He was a blackmailer, too?"

DeKok grinned crookedly.

"He didn't blackmail them at once. Marcel opened an account with the Ijsselstein Bank, a private account, and had the gentlemen deposit the expenses for his living merchandise directly into the account."

"Then what?" prompted Ans.

DeKok refilled the glasses and chose a croquet. This time his wife did not object. She encouraged the others to partake as well, while she refilled her glass with sherry. Vledder's eyes widened slightly. He had never seen DeKok's wife drink more than a single glass of sherry.

For awhile they ate and drank in silence. Then DeKok wiped his mouth with a napkin and continued without being urged.

"After Marcel set up the automatic deposits, everything progressed smoothly for a time. It was only a matter of time until scandals involving human trafficking were exposed in other countries. The resulting international scrutiny blocked Marcel's pipeline. When Marcel could no longer declare expenses, he began his systematic blackmailing. He also used his account at the bank for the proceeds of the blackmail. The gentlemen simply continued depositing. This time, of course, Marcel kept all the money for himself."

"That's why Darthouse denied the existence of the account," said Vledder, again stating the obvious.

"Exactly," answered DeKok blandly.

Vledder suddenly sat up straight.

"That's all very well, but it does not explain the murders, or why Father Hoogwoud was involved."

DeKok sighed and replaced his empty glass on the table.

"Father Hoogwoud," he began slowly, "is a strange man in many ways. To his family he was indeed a despotic patriarch, as Casper labeled him. But through his job as greenskeeper he showed an almost slavish subservience. It may be members of the club humiliated him, from time to time. In any case, the old man developed a strong hatred for the rich members of the club. When Marcel could no longer hide his wealth, Father Hoogwoud called him to account. Marcel told his father everything, frankly and without shame. In the beginning old Hoogwoud was angry, but later he relented. He chose to believe that the rich members of the club had enticed his son into a life of crime. He silently rejoiced when his son turned the tables on the quartet; he held these self-important rich people in the palm of his hand."

"He rejoiced?" repeated Vledder.

"Certainly. I'm convinced that he secretly admired his son for that."

"But there's still no motive," protested Vledder.

DeKok picked up a brochure.

"Acquired Immune Deficiency Syndrome," he read out loud.

"What role did AIDS play?" asked Ans, who had mostly been listening with bated breath.

DeKok spread his arms wide.

"The lead role," he answered. "AIDS and a growing hatred formed the motive for Father Hoogwoud."

"I don't understand," said Vledder.

DeKok lowered his head.

"It took a long time before I understood it myself. Only after I, literally, backed Leem far into a corner and he had told me everything did it become clear. Leem spilled about Marcel—the child smuggling, the parties. Look, the members of the quartet knew they were hostages to their blackmailer until the end of their days. It's rather obvious they discussed plans to rid themselves of Marcel. In spite of some discussion, for strictly practical reasons, they did not execute their plans. No doubt the gentlemen would still be conspiring, had fortunes not reversed. About a year ago, Marcel developed acute appendicitis. He immediately checked in at St. Matthew's Hospital."

"Dr. Hardinxveld," exclaimed Vledder.

"Yes," nodded DeKok. "Hardinxveld realized he had to quickly capitalize on the unique chance. There was a patient under his care, a young man who was infected with AIDS. It did not take long for the AIDS patient to die. Before he died, Dr. Hardinxveld took a sample of his AIDS-infected blood and injected it into Marcel."

"Murder."

"Yes, indeed, murder of a ghoulish kind. The surgeon knew Marcel would die…but not all at once. AIDS viruses divide and multiply slowly. It would take some time for Marcel to die. It was not a one-time act, but rather murder by installments."

"Reprehensible," said Mrs. DeKok. "And that from a doctor."

DeKok smiled gently.

"Hippocrates could never have known how many of his practitioners fill pages in the annals of crime."

He rubbed his chin.

"I think Marcel knew he'd contracted AIDS in the hospital. When he became really ill, later, he refused to go to a hospital. He did not trust the murderers in white coats, according to Casper."

"But how did Father Hoogwoud find out that Marcel had been infected with AIDS on purpose?"

"Pure coincidence and perfectly timed events are two necessary ingredients in our lives. Also, keep in mind that Hoogwoud kept a suspicious eye on the members of the quartet. One day they were together in the club house, enjoying their drinks. When Marcel and his blackmail became a subject of the conversation, Hardinxveld said it was just a matter of a few months. He was almost certain the AIDS virus would have done its work by then. He told them all about the injection. It was nice weather and the windows were wide open. Hoogwoud, who was working nearby, overheard bits of the conversation. When he got home that night, he asked his daughter to tell him about AIDS. That's when he learned that AIDS would, in most cases, result in death. He promised himself if Marcel died, he would have vengeance."

"That's why the killings started *after* Marcel died."

"Right."

"And who made the phone calls?"

"Marianne, the daughter. She acted upon instructions from her religious father, who chose the text."

"How did they incite their victims to go to those places in the middle of the night?"

"That was not very difficult. Hoogwoud said he had found the compromising photographs among Marcel's possessions. He said he did not want to keep such filth in his possession, and offered to return them with no strings attached."

"And they jumped at that?

DeKok nodded.

"And met their deaths," said Ans.

They remained silent for awhile, until Mrs. DeKok announced she was going to make coffee. She disappeared to the kitchen and DeKok poured out another measure of cognac for Vledder, Ans, and himself.

Then Mrs. DeKok came back with the coffee. They

drank their coffee while they talked about other subjects. Slowly the gruesome details of DeKok's narrative disappeared into the background.

Around eleven o'clock, Vledder and Ans said goodbye. Vledder asked Ans if he could drop her off, but she thanked him and declined gracefully.

"My boyfriend is picking me up," she said.

Mrs. DeKok saw the disappointment on his face. She intervened gently.

"You should have brought him along, my dear. When Dick's fiancé is in town, he always brings her to these little gatherings."

"Thank you, I will...if there is a next time," said Ans.

Vledder had the grace to blush.

"Do you mind going by the office on your way home?" asked DeKok.

"No, why?"

"Have them officially rescind the APB on Frankie and give him a call that he's a free man. Here is the number."

Vledder looked at the note DeKok gave him.

"Is that where he is?"

"Yes."

"You knew all along."

Laughing, DeKok shook his hand.

"We'll fight over that, tomorrow," he promised.

After his guests left, DeKok walked back to the living room. With a sigh of contentment he sank into his easy chair. He wanted to put his feet on the hassock before him, but his wife demonstratively sat down on it and looked him the eyes.

"Jurriaan DeKok," she said severely, "you're a liar."

DeKok gave her a measuring look.

"Why do you say that?"

She shook her head.

"Hoogwoud is *not* responsible for all three murders. At least one of the victims was killed by another."

DeKok looked puzzled, but did not fool his wife.

"Which one?" he asked innocently.

"Dr. Hardinxveld. Father Hoogwoud could never have committed the murder. He would have had to climb that steep stairway. He was physically incapable of that."

A smile played around DeKok's lips as he looked at his wife tenderly.

"They should hire you as a detective," he said with admiration.

His hand went to the pocket of his jacket, which hung on the back of his chair. The smile on his lips disappeared. Slowly he opened his hand and a revealed an exquisite brooch with a wide, glistening border, artfully filled with a finely worked filigree of silver.

"What is that?" she asked.

"Marianne's brooch. I found it under the corpse of Hardinxveld."

"*She* committed that murder."

DeKok nodded with a somber face.

"Marianne could not resist pressure from her father. By proposing a tryst, she enticed the doctor to meet her in the seldom used space below the heliport, where she bashed in his head."

Mrs. DeKok gave him a pitying look.

"And you let her go?"

The gray sleuth scratched the back of his head.

"I took the brooch to Father Hoogwoud. I placed it on the table in front of him. Then I made him a proposition."

Mrs. DeKok nodded slowly, her eyes filling with tears. "I understand," she said softly. "The father would assume all the guilt and you...you let Marianne go."

DeKok closed his hand.

"That's right."

"And where is Marianne at this time?"

DeKok shrugged.

"Far away. I think Africa, or maybe South America. In any case, she's in a place where a good nurse will be needed and appreciated."

"And that place was not, according to you, in jail."

DeKok gave his wife a loving look.

"You know me too well."

ABOUT THE AUTHOR

A. C. Baantjer is the most widely read author in the Netherlands. A former detective inspector of the Amsterdam police, his fictional characters reflect the depth and personality of individuals encountered during his near forty-year career in law enforcement.

Baantjer was honored with the first-ever Master Prize of the Society of Dutch-language Crime Writers. He was also recently knighted by the Dutch monarchy for his lifetime achievements.

The sixty crime novels featuring Inspector Detective DeKok written by Baantjer have achieved a large following among readers in the Netherlands. A television series, based on these novels, reaches an even wider Dutch audience. Launched nearly a decade ago, the 100th episode of the "Baantjer" series recently aired on Dutch channel RTL4.

In large part due to the popularity of the televised "Baantjer" series, sales of Baantjer's novels have increased significantly over the past several years. In 2001, the five millionth copy of his books was sold—a number never before reached by a Dutch author.

Known as the "Dutch Conan Doyle," Baantjer's following continues to grow and conquer new territory.

The DeKok series has been published in China, Russia, Korea, and throughout Europe. Speck Press is pleased to bring you clear and invigorating translations to the English language.

DeKok and the Geese of Death

Renowned Amsterdam mystery author Baantjer brings to life Inspector DeKok in another stirring potboiler full of suspenseful twists and unusual conclusions.

ISBN10: 0-9725776-6-1, ISBN13: 978-0-9725776-6-3

DeKok and Murder by Melody

"Death is entitled to our respect," says Inspector DeKok who finds himself once again amidst dark dealings. A triple murder in the Amsterdam Concert Gebouw has him unveiling the truth behind two dead ex-junkies and their housekeeper.

ISBN10: 0-9725776-9-6, ISBN13: 978-0-9725776-9-4

DeKok and the Death of a Clown

A high-stakes jewel theft and a dead clown blend into a single riddle for Inspector DeKok to solve. The connection of the crimes at first eludes him

ISBN10: 1-933108-03-7, ISBN13: 978-1-933108-03-2

DeKok and Variations on Murder

During one of her nightly rounds, housekeeper Mrs. van Hasbergen finds a company president dead in his boardroom. She rushes up to her apartment to call someone, but who? Deciding it better to return to the boardroom she finds the dead man gone.

ISBN10: 1-933108-04-5, ISBN13: 978-1-933108-04-9

DeKok and Murder on Blood Mountain

The trail of a recent crime leads Inspector DeKok to Bloedberg (Blood Mountain), Belgium, a neighborhood in Antwerp. A man was fished from the Scheldt River, and DeKok has been summoned to help with the investigation.

ISBN10: 1-933108-13-4, ISBN13: 978-1-933108-13-1

Boost

by Steve Brewer

Sam Hill steals cars. Not just any cars, but collectible cars, rare works of automotive artistry. Sam's a specialist, and he's made a good life for himself.

But things change after he steals a primo 1965 Thunderbird. In the trunk, Sam finds a corpse, a police informant with a bullet hole between his eyes. Somebody set Sam up. Played a trick on him. And Sam, a prankster himself, can't let it go. He must get his revenge with an even bigger practical joke, one that soon has gangsters gunning for him and police on his tail.

"…entertaining, amusing…. This tightly plotted crime novel packs in a lot of action as it briskly moves along."

—*Chicago Tribune*

"Brewer earns four stars for a clever plot, totally engaging characters, and a pay-back ending…."

—*Mystery Scene*

ISBN: 1-933108-02-9 | ISBN13: 978-1-933108-02-5

Killing Neptune's Daughter

by Randall Peffer

Returning to his hometown was something Billy Bagwell always dreaded. But he felt he owed it to Tina, the object of his childhood sexual obsession, to see her off properly. Even in death she could seduce him to her. Upon his return to Wood's Hole on Cape Cod, Billy's past with his old friends—especially his best friend, present day Catholic priest Zal—floods his mind with classic machismo and rite-of-passage boyhood events. But some of their moments were a bit darker, and all seemed to revolve around or involve Tina…moments that Billy didn't want to remember.

This psycho-thriller carries Billy deeper and deeper into long-repressed memories of thirty-five-year-old crimes. As the days grow darker, Billy finds himself caught in a turbulent tide of past homoerotic encounters, lost innocence, rage, religion, and lust.

"…the perfect book for those who fancy the darker, grittier side of mystery. A hit-you-in-the-guts psychothriller, this is a compelling story of one man's search for truth and inner peace."
—Mystery Scene

ISBN: 0-9725776-5-3 | ISBN13: 978-1-933108-05-6

speck

Nick Madrid Mysteries
by Peter Guttridge

No Laughing Matter

Tom Sharpe meets Raymond Chandler in this humorous and brilliant debut. Meet Nick Madrid and the "Bitch of the Broadsheets," Bridget Frost, as they trail a killer from Montreal to Edinburgh to the ghastly lights of Hollywood.
ISBN: 0-9725776-4-5, ISBN13: 978-0-9725776-4-9

A Ghost of a Chance

New Age meets the Old Religion as Nick is bothered and bewildered by pagans, satanists, and metaphysicians. Seances, sabbats, a horse-ride from hell, and a kick-boxing zebra all come Nick's way as he tracks a treasure once in the possession of Aleister Crowley.
ISBN: 0-9725776-8-8, ISBN13: 978-0-9725776-8-7

Two to Tango

On a trip down the Amazon, journalist Nick Madrid survives kidnapping, piranhas, and urine-loving fish that lodge where a man least wants one lodged. After those heroics, Nick joins up with a Rock Against Drugs tour where he finds himself tracking down the would-be killer of the tour's pain-in-the-posterior headliner.
ISBN: 1-933108-00-2, ISBN13: 978-1-933108-00-1

The Once and Future Con

Avalon theme parks and medieval Excaliburger banquets are the last things journalist Nick Madrid expects to find when he arrives at what is supposedly the grave of the legendary King Arthur. As Nick starts to dig around for an understanding, it isn't Arthurian relics, but murder victims that he uncovers.
ISBN: 1-933108-06-1, ISBN13: 978-1-933108-06-3

Peter Guttridge is the Royal Literary Fund Writing Fellow at Southampton University and teaches creative writing. Between 1998 and 2002 he was the director of the Brighton Literature Festival. As a freelance journalist he has written about literature, film, and comedy for a range of British newspapers and magazines. Since 1998 he has been the mystery reviewer for *The Observer*, one of Britain's most prestigious Sunday newspapers. He also writes about—and doggedly practices—astanga vinyasa yoga.

Praise for the Nick Madrid Mysteries

"Highly recommended."
—*Library Journal*, starred review

"…I couldn't put it down. This is classic Guttridge, with all the humor I've come to expect from the series. Nick is a treasure, and Bridget a good foil to his good nature."
—*Deadly Pleasures*

"Guttridge's series is among the funniest and sharpest in the genre, with a level of intelligence often lacking in better-known fare."
—*Baltimore Sun*

"…one of the most engaging novels of 2005. Highly entertaining…this is humor wonderfully combined with mystery."
—*Foreword*

"…Peter Guttridge is off to a rousing start…a serious contender in the mystery genre."
—*Chicago Tribune*

"[The] Nick Madrid mysteries are nothing if not addictively, insanely entertaining…but what's really important is the mix of good suspense, fast-and-furious one-liners and impeccable slapstick."
—*Ruminator*

"…both funny and clever. This is one of the funniest mysteries to come along in quite a while."
—*Mystery Scene*

For a complete catalog of our books please contact us at:

speck press
po box 102004
denver, co 80250, usa
e: books@speckpress.com
t & f: 800-996-9783
w: speckpress.com

Our books are available through your local bookseller.

speck